NOBODY'S ROAD

NOBODY'S ROAD
Olivia Hardy Ray

This book is a work of fiction. Names, characters, places and incidents are products of the author's imagination or are used fictitiously. Any resemblance to actual events, locales or persons, living or dead, is entirely coincidental.

ISBN: 978-1-64456-577-3 [paperback]
ISBN: 978-1-64456-578-0 [Mobi]

Library of Congress Control Number: 2022951577

SECOND EDITION

INDIES UNITED PUBLISHING HOUSE, LLC
P.O. BOX 3071
QUINCY, IL 62305-3071
indiesunited.net

Acknowledgements

I'd like to thank my beta readers and my fans who keep me writing and churning out new titles. Many thanks to Lisa Orban, publisher of Indies United for all she does. For the best covers ever, my appreciation goes to Dane at Ebook Launch and for an incredibly magical edit, thank you, Jayne Sullivan. Deep appreciation to Marianna Young for her faith in me as a writer, she's an exceptional cheerleader. Nobody's Road is a title that has been influenced by the nightly news and by a lovely little farmhouse I once owned in Delaware county, New York. Pindar Corners does exist, as does Nobody's Road but I can't tell you exactly where, just that I passed by one day and noticed, and thought: there's a book in thar road sign.

Books by Vera Jane Cook

Dancing Backward in Paradise
The Story of Sassy Sweetwater
Where the Wildflowers Grow
Lies a River Deep
Marybeth, Hollister & Jane
The Fourniers: Book One, When Hannah Played
Ragtime
The Fourniers: Book Two, Glamor Girl
The Fourniers: Book Three, The Memory of Music
(coming spring of 2022)

By Olivia Hardy Ray
(pen name of Vera Jane Cook)
Annabel Horton, Lost Witch of Salem
Annabel Horton and the Black Witch of Pau
Pharaoh's Star

NOBODY'S ROAD

OLIVIA HARDY RAY

INDIES UNITED PUBLISHING HOUSE, LLC

PART I:

THE LOST

CHAPTER ONE

My last memory from that time? That I was never to return to it.

As I ran to the rhythm of my breath, the beat of my heart provided the music of being alive. I took a hill, not as bad as it looked; steep but short. Chestnut was a single-lane road that cut through the back of town and led me onto Bishop Farm, where I picked up Maple Lane.

Dotted with sugar maples, Maple Lane wound out ahead of me, and like a lazy letter S, it snaked around for two long shaded miles. The sycamore trees had limbs that reached across the sky like Rorschach spills. The sweat on my back saturated my T-shirt, clinging like a second skin. The road had been nothing but dirt for over a hundred years; though the town kept threatening to pave it, they probably never will. A good part of the trail was a long narrow easement that took me past a mile of farmland. The dirt kicked up a gentle cloud of dust under my feet, soft and dry. The smell of freshly hoed hay and country pine lingered in the air.

Maple Lane begins and ends at Pindar Corners, a fork in the road with a blinking light. I picked up Robin's Nest Road from there, turning left at the traffic signal, as I always did.

1

How many times? I'm not sure. But I do know this, or thought I did: Robin's Nest is the road I lived on with my wife, Adina, and our children, Teddy, who was eight at the time and Lindsey, who hadn't yet turned six.

The scent of flower gardens hit me like a perfumed galaxy, overwhelmingly intense, from the abundance of flowers hidden behind picket fences and green bristly privacy bushes, odiferous and colorful. I saw irises, lilies and peonies that tilted in the breeze and slipped their scents toward me with flirtatious artistry.

Hundreds of times, I have picked up fragrances whispering from the mountains. You see, for me, one of the pleasures of jogging on a country road was catching smells. Even running through traces of horse manure carried in the wind, or the mysterious scents of unrecognizable plants and animals just behind the weeds, scents like that thrilled me. Might be perceived as such a small thing but it isn't, not when sweet, scented air was such a new thing for me.

I breathed in deeply. I took in passionflower vines climbing up trellises, a cacophony of color. Sometimes I can catch freshly cut grass and the sizzled scent of meat lingering on a barbeque, whetting my appetite for lunch.

Robin's Nest Road is paved and wide, and I liked it because it dead-ends; the only drivers who take it know exactly where they're going, and trucks are rare. Sometimes, I could run right down the middle with my arms outstretched. Feeling good for me was sweating hard ... feeling good for me was pushing up the last half mile, knowing I'd make it.

Jogging kept me centered — going at my own pace, my thoughts a free association of expression. No race to win, just moving through the silence of my mind, despite the rare chatter of birds or the occasional challenge of estival winds.

The only smells picked up back in New York City were mornings drenched in the stench of garbage and the rancid,

2

putrid odor of the homeless inhabitants who lined the streets of midtown. I tried not to think about that because I was one of the lucky ones: I wasn't there. And I was where I was because of the foresight of a man a lot smarter than I am. I was in Pindar Corners. A place you might want to be a hundred years from now, or maybe a hell of a lot sooner.

The reasons why I was there, in Pindar Corners, were too complex to fathom. Mistakes too great to lament. There was no sense dwelling on the past at all. Best to just breathe in deeply and try to let it go. Besides, there was nothing we could have done about it. No, nothing. Just concentrate on the aroma of gardenias, orchids and the delirium of lilac, and forget about everything else. We still had flowers, some species of birds, animals like skunks and rodents. We had life, and most of all, we had the solace and the surety of Pindar Corners.

However, the luxury of forgetting was the one thing I couldn't accomplish. I was a generation too late for that. And as I jogged that day, the sound of a distant gunshot jarred the aromatic titillation of my senses. So loud, it practically threw me off my feet. It certainly wasn't hunting season. I knew that well enough, but there were those who didn't give a damn about laws. Could have been someone wanting to frighten off a black bear. Then again, plenty of people liked target shooting in their back yards. It might have been some bored jerk shooting cans off a fence. Or it might have been one of the children. I don't think I was able to let in that fear. As far as I knew, there had only been one murder in Pindar Corners committed by a child. Maybe the shot I heard was just random and unintentional. That was my thought that day; that was my prayer.

In retrospect, I didn't have any other choices but the ones I made. But I must tell you, had I not been as sapient as I was, darkness would have spread over the earth like sudden blindness, a deep red blanket of blood would have covered over the green fields and masked the cerulean skies. The smörgasbord of summer flowers would have lain, like some rosaceous aftermath, buried in the memories of those still standing, silently beholding the iniquity.

Sounds harsh, I know. You don't believe me. But how could you know the truth? Well, let me enlighten you to the unfortunate and abysmal future that I alone curtailed. So much more violence might have come to pass were it not for the intervention of improbability, events I never dreamed possible, occurrences beyond my wildest imagination.

Anything out of the ordinary should always be treated with caution. It's certainly out of the ordinary to lose your life, wake up in a body that isn't yours and then return to wonder what madman created this impossible dilemma. Don't ever trust the predictability of recurring time or the logic of circumstance. The only sure thing is the creation of your own making – a lesson I learned the hard way.

On that early June day in Pindar Corners, I was in the prime of my life. A perfect day, and I was about to die. I turned my cap around to keep the bugs off my face and seconds later, I heard another shot. This time followed by a scream so shrill I might have cupped my ears.

Breathing hard, my entire body as scarlet as the blinking turn light behind me at the Corners, I reached into my waist belt for my water bottle. I took a few gulps and then doused my face. Another scream pierced the air, followed by dogs howling and barking, fracturing the mellifluous lilt of day. Despite the surreal quality of the screams, an impulse told me to follow the sound.

Confused, with little idea of where the hell I was going, I continued to run. After all, I was a hero. I was my own creation, as you are yours.

Another scream rang out from behind me. Disoriented, I pushed a button on my earphone and called my wife. "I heard someone scream," I said, barely giving her time to say hello. "I can't tell where it's coming from."

"What?"

"I heard someone scream," I repeated.

"Well, who? Do you know?"

"Sounded like a woman but I couldn't tell. Could have been a man. Could have been a child."

"Well, what do you think?"

"Well, I can't be sure."

"Where are you? I'll call the sheriff."

"I'm just up the road."

"On Robin's Nest?"

"Yeah, yeah," I said. "Get him here as fast as you can."

"Be careful, Harry. Come home right away. It may be one of them," she warned me. "There may be more of them than we thought, and they might be here, in Pindar Corners."

"I have to help, Adina … someone's being hurt. I heard gunshots. Maybe I can save someone's life. Do you think I should?"

"No, Harry, please, don't be a hero."

"I'll be careful, I promise. I promise, but I have to help. Someone has been shot."

I sprinted back the way I'd come in, toward the Corners. Just at the blinking turn light, I heard another scream – louder this time, more intense. There are four roads at the corners: Hawthorne, Spruce, Robin's Nest and, of course, Nobody's Road; but the scream wasn't likely to be coming from Nobody's Road because Nobody's Road goes back down toward county Route 12 and nobody lives on it. Oh, except for some notorious stranger who may or may not live on the road because no one ever sees him.

Gossip has it he doesn't actually live on the road but drives down there every now and then. Rumor is he bought up the land but didn't build a damn thing on it. The only thing on Nobody's Road is an old concrete storage unit. It's ugly: a concrete slab amidst mountains of green. Maybe this infamous phantom will tear it down and build something new, something grossly oval, like most of the newer houses. Adina calls them "eco-friendly rotten eggs." You'll soon see how stupid I was that day; Nobody's Road held all the answers.

I looked up quickly when I heard a woman's voice.

"Mr. Cooper, Mr. Cooper," she called. I heard her distress.

It was Old Lady Leeds. That wasn't really her name, of course, but Adina and I always referred to her as "Old Lady Leeds." If she had a first name, I had no idea what it was. She lived at the first house on Robin's Nest.

"I thought I heard someone screaming," she said as I ran up to her.

"I heard it too," I told her.

"You heard the shots, then?"

"Sure did."

She took off her garden gloves and we walked out onto the road, listening for the source of the gunshot. The uncomfortable thought occurred to me that we could be open targets for a maniac with a rifle.

"Where did the shots come from?" she asked.

"Don't know. I suggest you go inside, Mrs. Leeds."

"Might have been hunters," she said.

Another shot rang through the air, piercing the pale blue day and the birdsong expectation of early morning. I practically jumped into her arms.

"Get inside," I shouted and pushed her back. I ran toward the back of an old shack on the other side of the road. Maybe Adina was right and I should ditch the hero act; I wasn't sure just how brave I wanted to be. Maybe I'd hang out until I heard the sheriff's siren. Let the law do their job, no need for me to lose my life over it.

Old Lady Leeds ran back to the gate and called out my name.

"Get back!" I said sharply. "It's not hunters – it's not hunting season."

"Take Hawthorne," she called out to me. "I think the screams are coming from Hawthorne. I think the shots are coming from Hawthorne, too. Go quick, Mr. Cooper, someone needs help."

I looked at her as if she were crazy, but saw the desperation in her expression. She didn't want to die either and I guess I was her savior. Shit. What the hell? My day for intrepid acts. I turned and took the road behind me: Hawthorne.

"Help!" A man's voice rang out.

I stopped running but I didn't see anyone.

"Harry, is that you?"

He came out of the Lansing's back yard, popped his head right up over a Japanese Holly bush, as if he'd been hiding. It was Carl Lansing. He looked frightened. More than that, he looked petrified, sweat streaming down his face like an open hydrant.

"What the hell is it?" I asked. "I heard a woman scream," breathing hard, my shorts sticking to my legs.

"Yeah, you heard right." He took in a deep breath, his face as red as mine felt.

"What the hell is going on?" I asked. "Is it one of them, one of the children?"

Carl grabbed onto my T-shirt. "I can't believe it," he wept profusely and mournfully, like an animal in profound pain.

Whatever he was talking about, whatever he was afraid of, was inside his house: he kept pointing to it. I ran through the open gate and into the yard without thinking I could wind up with buckshot up my ass.

"Harry," Carl called. "Be careful, he's got a gun."

No shit, I thought.

As I got to the front door, Carl called again. "Try not to

7

hurt him, Harry."

Yeah, sure, why should I hurt someone trying to kill me? was my next thought.

The front door was wide open. Survival instinct told me not to go in, but I had to find out who needed help. After all, bravery is the makeup of a man. I looked back for Carl to see if he had followed behind me, but he wasn't wearing the makeup of a man that day.

I poked my head into the room carefully and listened hard. I heard nothing but a dog whimpering. I crouched down and crept inside on all fours to behind a chair and crouched down again. The dog continued to whimper. My heart pounded in my chest; each breath I took might be my last.

The stairs directly in front of the chair went straight up to the second landing, and shielded me from the landing. To my right was a wood stove: I picked up the iron poker. If someone attempted to ambush me, they'd surely get a swift stab in the gut.

Thirty seconds ticked by on the wall clock; I lifted my head to see if I could see anything. At least, I had the poker to fight off any surprise attacks.

Blood on the stairs was the first thing I saw. Still wet, which probably meant the killer was close. Then I saw the dog, a cute little terrier my kids liked to play with.

"Oscar," I called to the dog. I wanted him out of harm's way, fearing he would be shot, as well.

Oscar lay flat on his stomach. He refused to budge, protecting Katie.

"Oh, shit," I whispered. It took every ounce of self-control not to put my head down and weep.

Katie Lansing was Carl and Susan's five-year-old daughter, and she was dead. I didn't even have to touch her. I knew by her face, most of which was missing.

Frantic, I looked around, breathing heavily, my heart

about to burst out of my chest, certain the killer could hear every breath I took. Clearly, a monster was loose in this house. Shaking so much, I felt useless, unable to wield my only weapon should I have to.

I gathered my courage as best I could and slowly started up the stairs, the poker tightly in my hand. But there wasn't a killer in the world that would have taken me seriously, because I was bawling loudly, like a baby.

On the landing lay Susan Lansing, Carl's wife and little Katie's mother, slumped over and covered in blood. She was dead too, no question about it.

Why the hell didn't Carl protect his family?

The realization of who might have done this washed over me. The next question was whether I could raise that poker in defense. Could I strike a child? But I had to raise it now and I would strike. I would kill him. I might not want to, but I would.

Quietly, I eased back down the stairs. Petrified. Every nerve ending screamed that this monster, crouched in a corner, waited for me. I wished I were closer to the open front door.

Both feet back on level ground, I bolted toward the door. Katie and Susan were gone, the best thing to do was to save myself.

I heard the sound as he came out from behind the drape and spun on reflex when I heard his voice.

"Galactigo. Galactigo, stop, or I'll shoot you dead!"

Corey Lansing pointed a twelve-gauge shotgun at me. Carl and Susan's ten-year-old son. He smiled as if the dead bodies of his mother and sister weren't lying in pools of blood.

"Corey?" I whispered.

"Who the hell are you?" he said. "You're not Galactigo."

The blast from the shotgun in his hand blew me off my feet.

9

"Another one," I whispered, right before my body shattered into pieces. Everything went black. Time stopped, but I heard my heartbeat … *thump* … *thump* … *thump*. Someone called me … then nothing …

I was a whole new man, lost in an echo to a history that never knew my name.

You don't believe me? It is the future. It is the truth.

CHAPTER TWO

New worlds are created out of the despair of the old. Then before you know it, tails have become heads, Goliath weak and childhood bemoaned as a cautionary journey of freaks. What mind could have created it so, you might ask? I have no answer, only the tale.

In the year 2045 I was thirty years old. I did not see my world as unusual, because as far as I was concerned, there had never been any other way; there had never been any other possibility but the one I experienced as reality. The Brain counts on this naivety.

By 2045 truth was forbidden, and so, we were fed lies. I didn't discover the depth of our misfortune until after I met Adina. I was too much a part of the system, too ingrained in the acceptance of deception to consider that once, not so long ago, society was not a monotone, not a series of blinks and clicks on a keyboard, not a dimming of the sun that left the earth in shadows.

I want you to know that the deterioration of spontaneity and laughter didn't disappear in the blink of an eye: it was a process, a deliberate process. I might add: slowly, over time.

The world was too busy to notice what was happening, I

assume. Some people were too intent on survival, others too focused on greed to recognize their loss of control of everything that made them human. Therefore, it happened … surreptitiously … before armies could be formed to prevent the transformation. The enemy was an inconspicuous malignancy.

In 2045, the world was a place in which leisure was obsolete. Work was all there was. Wealthy children were left alone with servants by parents held captive by whatever function they fulfilled for The Brain. There weren't any adults with the time or inclination to nurture children, except for our servants, many of whom were robotic. As a society, we had no choice. This was just the way it had come to be.

The Computer Project educated Children of the wealthy to be masters at their trade. Computer Project children replicated a superior society, one in which there were no dysfunctions, no mediocrity and no mistakes.

The Computer Project taught me that once upon a time there was a middle class. My world included no such thing. In my class, and by that, I mean, *wealthy class*, no one was denied an education. All wealthy babies born in America were Computer Project babies, considered the chosen ones.

Less fortunate children of the poor were put into institutions and raised the old-fashioned way, by teachers and state-appointed nannies. These children graduated into the military or into civil service, bureaucratic and mundane work. Some of them toiled away in restaurants, bars and hotels, their destinies determined by their IQs. Mostly, they competed with holographs and robots for those jobs. But their propensity for certain abilities could be considered. The children of the poor might have remained in the institutions, teaching, if they requested it, and if they had no history of independence that would compel them to turn out to be passionate insurgents.

Bullshit was forbidden for children of the poorer classes,

no rabble-rousing tolerated. They messed up, they went to an island on one of our few remaining oceans, where they stayed for the rest of their lives, and no one much gave a shit if they killed each other off, which is exactly what happened to most of them.

Education in America had been a failure, ergo, this old methodology was tossed to the poor like a bone; at least it was something.

Privileged children, like me, were referred to as Computer Project Babies. We could choose our professions if we passed the necessary tests. If we failed, we were relegated to more menial positions. I became a grossly overworked and severely edited cartoonist, creator of the alien super-hero, Mandero, archenemy of Galactigo, the very enemy Cory was pursuing when he shot me.

The compassionate Mandero I first created became, by directives I could not avoid, a predator, a killer who gobbled up puppy dogs for breakfast and destroyed his enemies with slow-burning torches, taking slices of skin for souvenirs and feeding the heads of his conquests to his pet lions. Not my idea, but immensely popular.

The government of The Brain paid us large annual compensations. Why not? We received a rigorous education, completely structured by the Computer Project, and we gave back over eighty percent of our lives.

Over five hundred professions were offered to graduates of the Computer Project. With this privilege, we had to make lifelong commitments to our chosen fields. We received college education privileges for our children and given housing, posh benefits and lavish investments. All of us worked for The Brain, so you might say the government employed us.

My parents were wealthy courtesy of generations of inheritance, from decades of wealth, and I was considered privileged at birth. Since society has only two classes, we ruled. While The Brain employed us, the lower classes worked for us, maintained our lives and had little of their own, with no opportunity to advance. Mostly because we needed them to handle everyday necessities such as cooking and cleaning, or manning garages, farming and such, as well as keeping our robots well maintained. If our servants rebelled, they were sent to jails. Many times, they were shot on the spot as "problematic citizens."

I applied for my wife in 2045. Since upper-class heterosexual women were a scarcity, I was lucky to have this option. I had graduated from Penn State Virtual five years earlier, and my parents had been requesting my marriage for years. The Brain finally gave permission for us to receive a file on potential wives for me.

"Act fast, Harry," Mother said. "Before all the good ones in your file get deleted."

I knew that details of many of the women in my file would also go to other men who had recently received permission to marry. As the women were selected, the file would be transferred back to The Brain and held on drives called "Appropriated Females." If I didn't act fast enough, I might not be able to fatten my file for another five years.

I had always been close to my parents and didn't object when they offered to help me find a wife. I lived at home because the only housing afforded single people were small three hundred square foot studios. I didn't feel I needed to exert my independence. My parents had two floors right off Central Park West and my bedroom was on the second floor, all nine hundred square feet of it. I could easily escape to the privacy of my nine-hundred-square-foot apartment and play my rat-kill music loud; my parents never heard it.

We worked on the file together, well, at least, Mother and I did. My father was indifferent, just said he'd give me his blessing, which was a joke. There were no blessings in our world.

Mother and I argued about the physical appearance of this one or that one, temperament and IQ, of course, which was far more important to Mother than to me. It was probably a mistake to allow my mother the liberty of helping me choose my bride. Undoubtedly, I should have kept her out of something so personal, but we didn't have many friends in our society and I valued my parents. I had to stand my ground though, before Mother paired me off with one of the old ones. Old women had been in huge supply, ever since the popularity of female babies in the 2030s – when choosing the sex of one's children was in vogue.

"I want a brunette, tall, smart and extroverted," I insisted.

Mother disagreed. "I know redheads are rare, and therefore expensive, darling. But think how nice it would be to have children with candy-colored hair."

"I don't want children with candy-colored hair," I said and went back to my search. I heard Dad chuckle. Marriages cost the pairing couples huge donations to The Brain, and women with red hair, large breasts and little DNA potential for physical abnormalities were worth donations of several hundred thousand.

The Brain had filled my file with fifty possibilities. Unfortunately, whatever taste in women The Brain had did not coincide with my own. I had already exhausted half the choices sent me, a bunch of ordinary-looking women behind the wheels of their Zippies, our popular sport cars powered by high-speed batteries. Or they looked like perfectly bored bimbos who had spent too much time with their plastic surgeons.

Then I brought up an image that intrigued me.

"Here, look at this one," I shouted. I maximized the image and double-clicked on the digital features of Adina Cordova. Her face filled the sixty-inch screen while my heart pounded in overtime. Her smile was so captivating, as if she knew secrets I'd never be privy to. Her wavy dark hair ended at her chin. Her eyes were large, dark ovals, at once both sad and lively.

"Beautiful," I whispered.

I refused to look at my mother. Instinctively, I knew she'd disapprove. I'd pulled up an esthetical angel, much too captivating for my mother's idea of good wife material. I quickly brought up her résumé despite the argument that would follow.

"Adina Cordova graduated from the Computer Project top of her class," I said.

"Adina Cordova?" Her name seemed to be of interest to my father. He jumped out of his chair and came to stand beside me.

"She's a knockout, Dad."

He didn't answer me, his expression distressed.

"Not really," he finally said.

Mother was immediately suspicious, or at least that's what I thought at the time.

"Smart women can be something of a bore," Mother said.

"Her degree was in journalism, Mother, not in the history and characteristics of the African Bat Bug."

My parents eyed one another, one of those looks between them I was always unable to interpret.

"Uh-oh," I thought I heard my mother utter.

But I found Adina's background extremely interesting. She had lived abroad during her teenage years while her father worked as a chef in Milan. It seems Europe treated Mr. Cordova like a king, extensively praised for his excellence in the culinary arts. Mrs. Cordova had been a dancer but had recently suffered a breakdown after The Brain's subversion and erasure of the Arts in Europe. When the Cordovas protested the infiltration and dismissal of the arts by Britain and America's Computer Educational system, they were deported and returned to the States in 2038.

Admitted into Columbia, Adina had graduated with honors. As a child, she'd grown up not far from me, but she was three years younger, which might explain why we hadn't come across each other on those rare occasions that The Brain allowed social integration.

"Where is she from again, Harry?" Mother asked.

"She's American born. But her father lived and worked in Europe for a while. They were kicked out of Italy. She was raised not far from us, practically down the block."

"Sounds iffy to me, Harry. Her expectations might be extremely high, and the whole family are rabble-rousers. I know that for a fact."

It appeared to me that Dad was making a real pitch to keep me away from Adina.

"Your father's right," Mother added quickly. "Don't think with your penis, dear."

I heard Dad chuckle again as he returned to his chair on the other side of the room. Despite his chuckle, I sensed uneasiness.

"But I like her," I said to them. "She's different. Something about her I just like."

"You don't know her yet," Mother said.

"Look at her eyes," I responded.

"But are you compatible, darling?" Mother stared at the digital image before her. "I like the other one, with that engaging smile."

I shrugged. Mother liked the mousey one – heart surgeon, high IQ, and a face I'd seen in an old comic strip about cave people.

I clicked back on Adina. "This one is more petite."

Drooling by now, I wiped my mouth inconspicuously. This gal was a knockout and Mother feared I wouldn't attract her. I was Harry all right, but no handsome Harry, that was for sure.

"Well, she is nice, maybe a bit too pretty though. Pretty women can be a bother."

Dad winked. "You can say that again."

I hadn't expected my mother to get it. I threw up my hands. "Mother, do you want me to search the homely file? I mean, I know the dogs are cheaper, but I really don't want an arf arf, if you don't mind."

"No, of course not, darling. If you like this woman, ping her … get your compatibility tested … see if she likes you."

Mother's eyes traveled back to my father. I couldn't tell what they were thinking, but each seemed to be able to read the other's thoughts.

"You bet," I said as I brought up her address file and sent out a quick imail to The Brain, requesting a date with her.

Much to my surprise, my father knocked on my door later that evening. I was nearly asleep.

"Son?"

I sat up in bed and switched on the lamp. He sat on the edge of my bed and stared at me.

"You know that I never want to see you hurt …" My father is a large man and I felt myself tipping from his weight. When I was a child, I fell out of bed a few times when he came to say goodnight, but that was before I learned to scurry to the middle before he sat.

As if he sensed my discomfort, he rose to his feet and paced back and forth. I wondered what he had to say.

"Father, I have a right to pick a woman of my choosing, not one that you and Mother prefer. We agreed to that. I said I'd ask for feedback, not ultimatums."

"It isn't that, Harry. It's this girl … she will be different."

I shook my head in disbelief. "What are you saying?"

I heard him sigh and return to the edge of my bed. I tipped up again and slid to the middle of the mattress before he tossed me to the carpet.

"She will corrupt you, son."

18

Unable to believe what I'd just heard, I jumped out of bed and paced around the room. My father stared at me wearily.

"Just what the hell are you talking about, Father?"

"She was raised believing in the absurd and the ridiculous. Her father is a real nut case. The whole family is trouble."

"What are the absurd and the ridiculous?" I asked, standing before him in defiance.

My father leapt to his feet and the mattress nearly flew to the ceiling. He banged his hands together and the lamp on my nightstand rattled.

"You can't survive being a rebel, Harry. Not in this world anyway, not here."

"What?" I looked at him in disbelief. "I'm not a rebel."

"That girl is."

"What are you talking about, you don't even know her."

It was at that point that my father went to the computer and turned it on. He typed in several logins and bypassed several codes before he arrived at a webpage. I almost fell asleep waiting for him to find what he wanted.

"Listen to this," he finally said, snapping me awake.

He read aloud from what he had pulled, which appeared to be a newsletter:

"'One in five now is killing. The Brain is responsible. The Brain spreads a disease that must be eradicated. Our children are dying from that disease. What maggots will walk the earth tomorrow? What horror walks the earth today? Be strong and educate your children. Be strong and educate yourself. Conquer this malignancy. Our minds have atrophied, our philosophers are silenced, and machines that have no humanity murder our souls.'"

My mouth fell open as I stared at him. "What the hell was that?"

"It was written by Adina Cordova."

"So what?" I said. "She's entitled to her opinion, though I'm not sure what it is."

"Harry, Harry," My father grabbed me in his arms. "There isn't room for truth. There is only room for self-preservation."

I broke from my father's grasp. "Look, let's just see if we like each other. You're jumping the gun."

"Your mother is crying in her room," my father said.

"I'm sorry about that, but I don't understand the great drama you two are embroiled in just because I have a physical attraction to Adina Cordova. Mother is overreacting, as are you."

"Perhaps."

"You want to marry me off to an arf, don't you?"

"No, no, no. It isn't that at all, son. We want you to be safe."

"Look, I've requested a date with her. Let's see how it goes. Maybe we won't like each other. Perhaps it won't be anything more than a rough fuck," I said.

He nodded quietly, kissed me on the cheek and left the room, but not before adding that he hoped we'd recoil from each other.

Recoil? I wondered. Who would recoil from that face?

I didn't understand either of my parents' reactions, and I was furious. But one thing for sure, it wouldn't stop me from pursuing the only woman, out of a file of fifty, who didn't look as though she'd just finished a foul lunch.

CHAPTER THREE

I didn't get a response for over a week and decided my application to date and possibly marry Adina had been denied. Perhaps someone else had requested her. But much to my surprise, at midnight one evening, I heard my Sonic berry bling. Ms. Adina Cordova had sent me an email. It read:

> You seem interesting, Harry. I received your file just today. I am told you've requested a proposal of marriage. I must admit, I'm not easy to please. Most of the men I meet are very dull, even a bit mean-spirited; a sign of the times, I suppose. I don't really approve of going through The Brain for a husband. How does that suit you? Will you consider me a troublemaker or just plain stupid? Maybe there isn't any other way to pair off and I'm just being difficult. I was beginning to think I'd have to travel back to Italy for a mate, though I'd never get a

visa now, not with all these new mandates from The Brain. So, perhaps I'm fated to be an Old Maid. I'll make the best of it then, with my cat and my knitting. But before committing myself to a husbandless future, I'll give you a try. I hope you don't disappoint me, Harry. I've been feeling terribly forlorn, but that's not unusual. Sometimes, I feel as if love will evade me forever. Do you know love, Harry? Have you ever felt it? Perhaps not here in this crowded city of strangers where everyone seems to live behind their Sonics: so sorrowful and distant. And behind the distraction of Sonics and Mighty Me iPods – an endless dark hole, nothing but that. No one there, no one home. What makes our world so morose? Is it too much isolation?

My answer was brief, but I was afraid to say more. This was surely a woman who would cut me off at the balls if I dared say the wrong thing. I mean, I had never communicated with anyone like her before.

Sweet Adina, I like you already, not just for your obvious good looks but also for the way you think. I've been bored by the women I've met. I want to soar like an eagle when I caress a woman's eyes with my own. You've already given me hope for something more than mediocrity. Yes, I agree, we live in such a bleak world nowadays. No fault of our own, I guess,

just a byproduct of progress. But I, too,
long for something else, some
brightness at the end of the day, some
laughter – a woman with spirit and
substance. I won't disappoint you either,
I promise.

I had to wait another whole week before she replied.
Like most people, we worked until midnight four days a
week and our days began at eight in the morning, so we were
clearly tired. It didn't help either to be on so many drugs. We
took them to induce sleep, and then again, we took them for
energy the next day. Drugs probably produced more income
for The Brain than Zippies and gambling combined.

011001110011101110110001001101111011001000111001001001111011110011001100100100000001010010011011101110110000101100100

Dear Harry, I'm sufficiently intrigued.
You see, I left my laughter behind me
and I have been unable to find it again. I
yearn for it now, especially after hearing
from you. Oh, make me laugh, Harry,
bring me to my knees with it; make my
belly ache with it. Open my heart with it.
If you are not the man for the job, I will
swim all the way back to an earlier age
when people still had choice. Let The
Brain find me there in my time machine,
let The Brain recognize me amid the
blithesome song of the living.

I felt my head spin. This woman was like no other I had
ever known, but I had known so few. As I said, dating was
difficult; there was so much red tape. Sex was easy to find
though, considering the number of bars in the city, but
finding the right woman was arduous. Men of my generation
didn't go to bars to find wives; we went to bars to find

companionable copulation. If we didn't meet a possible mate on our jobs, we were subject to The Brain's control. The Brain could even refuse us a mate of our choice if it were of the opinion we could procreate more productive children with someone else, or children of a particular ethnicity, since very few people of color could populate without The Brain's permission. Since the Caucasian act of 2028, The Brain mandated majority status once again for Caucasians, and therefore, controlled all other births until the appropriate Caucasian numbers were reached.

We were all pretty much relegated to the bars for sex, but there was never any expectation of anything else. I didn't enjoy the activity of what came to be termed "luck fucks" or "rough fucks" because of the harsh competition to snare women, to snatch them away from other men, or to be snatched – hardly a compliment, and no more interesting than being accosted by poor females hoping to entice me into marriage by eagerly offering me their secondhand vaginas.

"Don't get your hopes up, Harry," my father said. "Women rarely mean what they say."

Father was still expending a great deal of energy in persuading me to apply for a new file of women.

I glanced at my mother, who seemed in agreement with Father's remark. It was obvious that both were still hoping to talk me out of pursuing Adina. Mother said things like, "Can't trust the rise in a storm, Harry, it's unpredictable. And her eyes are shifty."

"Is that true?" I asked my mother. "Women rarely mean what they say?"

"We are not bound by truth," she said. "What does it mean to be truthful, Harry?"

I shook my head; I didn't have an answer. The Computer Project had taught us that everything was a concept and only a concept – like God, love, passion. Truth, then, was irrelevant because it was subjective and always changing. I looked at my indignant mother.

"I'll adopt her truth then and it will become my truth and it won't matter that women are untruthful because everything she says will be true to me." I stood firm and stared down my father. I'd picked up Mother's indignant demeanor and the air of superiority gave me confidence.

"Then you'll wind up being pussy-whipped, with no truth of your own." My father gave me an unyielding look, nothing I could interpret fully.

"Then dominance will be part of her charm, and submission, part of mine," I said willfully.

His laughter followed me as I took to the stairs. "Charm wears thin after a while," he called up to me.

My computer screen lit up as I entered my room. The screen was like an oval earth throwing its messages around my head and reflecting off the walls. Automatically, I pointed at my mail, the tiny envelopes flipped open and I glanced at them through the soft blue light of my computer.

My father was trampling on my last nerve. Suddenly, he had so much to say. He barely spoke at all unless reacting to something he'd heard on his weird news channel; then he could talk for hours, berating our society, calling us the offspring of fools, anthropoids of nearsighted drones and brain-dead opportunists. I rarely listened to him, but I did find it strange that he'd be so upset with Adina when he, too, detested The Brain.

Mother was always more attuned to my needs, and so I was grateful she finally approved of Adina. Well, not so much approved, but rather acquiesced to my final decision. She still thought Adina had shifty eyes and was overweight. "She looks like she's one hundred twenty pounds, Harry. She looks like she's on a sugar diet."

Adina and I had written to each other for weeks by this time. We'd shared pod drops, huge images of ourselves that made me wonder if she could tell that I was short and had one crooked tooth on the side of my smile. But she told me I was cute, so maybe not. Much to my amazement, "cute" was a term I now embraced, though I had always hated it; it tainted my childhood – my cheeks still stung from the myriad people who pinched me and called me "cute."

Well, times change. Cute seemed to define us both. As gorgeous as Adina appeared, I saw a kittenish quality, an allure I found becoming, a woman detached, to a point, from her own beauty.

I was getting to know her through her imails, but was soon frustrated by them. Of course, she was an interesting person, so much so that I wanted to know more about her each day, but I wanted to be in her real time and space. So far, she was beyond any fantasy I'd ever had about the woman of my dreams. Instinctively, I knew I could talk to her. She looked beyond the mundane repetition of our lives into other possibilities … such as the element of surprise and mystery. The soul file we were not permitted to access suddenly filled me with curiosity because Adina referred to it often. She said there were elements in the soul file as likely as sunsets and thunder. I certainly hoped The Brain wouldn't censor her.

When we weren't permitted to access it, I was desperate to ask Adina how she knew what was in the soul file. I assumed she'd been able to read its entirety in Europe before the Europeans banned it as well.

Since there were random readings of our imails, I couldn't ask her anything that might subject either of us to be reprimanded and deleted from each other's files. But it seems I'd never get the opportunity to ask her anything of value anyway; The Brain was not giving us the time to date. Fortunately, we were both coming upon brief respites in our schedules at work, respites given every so often to workers who never got sick.

During this difficult time, Adina said it was an opportunity for us to get to know one another through our words and feelings. She sent me at least three imails a day while we waited for our work respites. Those imails were like foreplay, setting off so many enzymes in my head and my eager penis that I didn't need the Ambien we all took at bedtime to induce sleep. I welcomed dreams, cloudy sweet excursions into sex more stimulating than any virtual porn site I'd visited. If Adina only knew the positions of pleasure she took in the fantasies of our first date.

01.001.1.1.001.1.01.1.1.01.1.0001.001.1.01.1.1.1.01.1.001.0001.1.1.1.001.001.001.1.1.01.1.1.001.1.001.000001.01.001.001.1.01.1.1.01.1.00001.01.1.001.00

Something is missing, isn't it, Harry? I read that it wasn't always like this, that the streets weren't as crowded, the poor not as threatening. I read that people traveled without having to apply for instate visas that took months to acquire. Now that I'm back in the country of my birth, I won't be allowed to live abroad again. We had to come back when Father and Mother protested Computer Educations for Europeans. As hateful as it sounds, I often think it wasn't worth the trouble, a terrible mistake. We should have remained in Europe and kept our mouths shut. Everything changed the moment we landed in New York. We came back to all these new rules that are like terminal maladies. But once upon a time, people were free in America, Harry. I read somewhere that we didn't ask The Brain for our mates, nor did we need approval to love. We met with our eyes and our emotions followed like ripples that grew into waves.

But it doesn't pay to be silent, does it? Europe has adopted the ways of America and they drown us, as well, in this current of disaster they have followed. We're lucky America allowed us back in, we might have been sent to the Middle East, where white outcast Americans are rendered slaves for the wealthy.

I wondered why she didn't fear retaliation from The Brain. Father was right; this girl was a rebel and clearly fearless.

Oh, Adina, I read today that men once wore top hats and courted women with roses. Isn't that something! Their shoes were wing-tipped and their manners soft. You make me feel like a gentleman of old, wanting to stand when you enter a room, open doors as you pass. Oh, Adina, you've made me a suitor, suer, a wooer and a romantic. How good it feels to feel so inclined.

01.0011.1001.101.1.101.10001.001.101.1.1.101.1001.0001.1.1.001.001.001.1.101.1.1001.1.001.000000.101.001.001.101.1.1.101.1.10001.101.1001.00

About a month after I'd first pinged her, I got the best news of my life. I had just returned from a run in Central Park and somehow knew my world was about to flip upside down, excited about some unknown occurrence that hadn't yet happened, but was about to. Adina would later tell me that I was psychic that day. I'd have laughed my head off if she'd mentioned it then. How times change.

I flew up the stairs when I got home. I figured whatever

28

was causing my sense of elation would surely be found on my computer.

My computer filled my room like a spaceship, like a planet lit up in blues and greens. There it was, an imail from The Brain, flashing in red lights that usually initiated anxiety, for no one really wanted to hear from The Brain. But this was good news; I had been released from evening hours for one whole week. I hoped Adina had also been released. I knew she had applied. I scanned down several more imails, ads mostly. I paid no attention to the others when I saw her name.

> Meet me at Maxwell's on Columbus at 8:00 P.M. I'll be at the bar waiting to be enchanted. Only have to work eight hours a day this week. How fine!

And that's how it all began. I'll never forget the first time I saw her. I became an immediate fool. I tried to ground my emotions, to keep the spirit I didn't know I had from flight. It was simply too frightening to just let go, but when push came to shove, I had no choice.

CHAPTER FOUR

I looked over the crowd at the bar. Maxwell's was a hot spot, and filled with people. The lighting was dim, mostly candlelight, since even low-energy high-wattage bulbs were prohibited. Several women smiled in my direction. I didn't smile back. I was looking for her. My eyes traveled the room; without a trace of Adina, panic set in. Increasingly frustrated, I wondered if she'd be a no-show.

The usual animal survival of the fittest atmosphere prevailed at Maxwell's. So many had taken pay cuts for the extra hours or earned them through several excruciatingly long work days. The music was unbearably loud, so much so that the glasses rattled on the shelf above the bar. Women with barely any clothes on, the style of the day, groped the crotches of men they found attractive, and men practically fornicated with women who stood near them in the thronged maze at the bar.

I might have left after several stretched poses on the toes of my feet provided not a glimpse of Adina. Then, quite by accident, a woman who sat near the door caught my eye and probably witnessed my rendition of the old ballets we watched for comic relief at lunch. The Brain called old ballets and *Ozzie and Harriet* television reruns from the 1950s, "stress reduction."

Enveloped in one of those tight black jumpsuits popular that year, sipping a martini, she was much more beautiful than any digital image. A profile shot of the perfect woman – glamorous, yet playful, just as I had suspected. Unfortunately, there was a tall, thin, and incredibly handsome man leaning over her, salivating like a horny dog. Furious – as if I had a right to be jealous – my anger gave me courage and I walked behind Mr. Movie Star and grinned at Adina.

She slid her eyes toward me, as if able to read my thoughts. The minute I met her steady gaze, sweat beaded on my brow, trickled down my back and armpits. She was not petite at all. She was rather tall, maybe even taller than me, which isn't saying much because I'm short for a guy. Her breasts were obviously large. That is to say, her breasts were obvious. I stared at them, two beckoning bounteous boobs. I made a mental note not to ogle them all evening, however challenging that might prove.

We'd flash dated for weeks, exchanging digitals and webcam smiles and all those hokey notes, but now the real moment was here, flesh to flesh, eye to eye. I worried she wouldn't like me close up. I'm what some girls would call attractive, but never a man's man, like Mr. Movie Star, still smiling at Adina, showing his white shark teeth.

"Excuse me," I said and forced myself in front of the movie star.

I'd always wanted to be considered a man's man, but unlike the movie star, my two front teeth are large and slightly bucked. My deep dimples make me look like a perpetual ten-year-old, and I still wear glasses, which makes me look like an antique, but glasses have come back in style recently, and I like them. My eyes are light and, therefore, sensitive to the sun. The heavy plastic lenses protect me from resembling a pink-eyed bunny rabbit, and since we no longer have much of an ozone layer around the planet, they also keep me from going blind; all in all, they're quite useful. They're rather nice glasses too, and I think more people should wear them instead of those overly filtered contacts. My glasses are small, round and tortoiseshell, fashioned after a style popular at the early part of the century.

My hair is my best feature if you like curly hair. I wear it combed back off my face and it's so black it shines without gel. Women seem to like my hair because they're always roughing it up. I wore my favorite shirt that night, grey and tight around my chest. My slacks were tight too. I wanted her to notice I had a rather good build for a short guy, so I slung my jacket over my shoulder and stood there like a rock star, a short rock star, perhaps, but still pretty electric guitar rocky.

I must have looked a complete moron posing as a rocker after all those tippy-toe ballet stretches.

"Adina?" I mouthed to her amused grin.

She continued to grin as she nodded. I imagine she had the same thought; only a complete twerp would stand on his toes.

Truly, I have little experience with women. I could only do what I thought would be appropriate; so, at that point, I gaped at her. I thought I'd shared a sexy smile, but she told me later that I was drooling. Her facial expression suggested she'd already swept me up and spat me out. It surprised me to be so nervous, but there I was, a regular sweaty, drippy version of Mr. Right.

Firing the movie star a threatening stare, I sauntered closer and flashed a smile at Adina. The movie star walked away after he treated me to a death-wish nod.

"Grrrrrrr," I said as I slipped in beside her. Using my sensitive olfactory modality, I sniffed in the crisp, cool scent of her rather intoxicating body oil.

She raised an eyebrow and stared at me like an unwanted rip in her nice sweater.

"Don't tell me you're Harry Cooper?"

"In the flesh," I said. I tried to avoid grinning; my overbite contradicted the impression I was trying to portray.

"Do you expect me to growl back at you?" she asked.

I stammered a bit. In the attempt to be suave, flirtatious and irresistible, I came off like a bad salesman.

"That was my way of saying you're beautiful." I blushed; not very manly of me. I was blowing it. Perhaps it was too dark in the bar for her to see that my cheeks looked like cranberries.

She stared at me as if I were a cretin. There was a whole file on impressing women, and I had neglected to reread it that year. Actually, how many years had it been since I read the chapter on first impressions ... at least five? If I could have kicked myself, I would have.

"Should we get a table?" I asked as I pulled on my belt loops and hacked up my slacks.

"Don't you want a drink?"

"Sure, sure," I said and put my foot up on the rim of her stool. The smell of her hair had the effect of the rust cleaner everyone was sniffing. I simply wanted to close my eyes and lie somewhere near her luscious boobs. Instead, I ordered two martinis and stole but a glance at her high peaks.

By the time we got to our table, I had bored her with football and the mechanics behind old car engines. I droned on and on, giving her little opportunity to comment, had she wanted to. It was as if I could think of nothing to say that would interest her and I pontificated on everything that wouldn't. I could have talked about rat-kill music, The Brain's most recent ban on the Special Olympics, even the weather ... but my mind was below my belt.

"Remember the old Fords and Chryslers?" I asked.

She shook her head. "I've no use for antiques. I've been driving a Zippie for years."

"Oh," I said. I hated Zippies. They couldn't replicate the charm of the old gas guzzlers. Although outlawed for decades, we still kept them hidden in garages and had car chases on old, abandoned roads by the deserted beaches of Long Island, further polluting the air with bootleg gasoline.

"You don't like football either, do you?" I asked.

"Hate football."

"Well, what do you like?"

"Food."

"Oh, yes." We read the menu on the table computer. "Would you like the sound?" I asked.

Sound was good for ordering and would stall for time and give me the opportunity to think of some other way to put my foot in my mouth.

The evening specials were read aloud, and you had to really listen as they flipped past quickly. I watched her punch the audio for specials.

"Potato au gratin with steak smothered in onions and sautéed in sweet butter and truffle oil for the ladies ... and for the adventurous seafarer, Chilean sea bass with capers, steamed in sherry wine. Try it, gentlemen, it's soft as her shoulder, succulent as her kiss," read some guy with a lisp.

Adina ran her tongue over her lips while I perspired more profusely under my nose, a rather small, upturned thing that Mother always said was adorable. It did nothing to hide the sweat and made me look like a leprechaun, or one of those goddamned fairies that run amuck in the forest of a children's fairy tale.

I remembered her profile, or at least what The Brain had permitted me to see. I'd memorized it verbatim. She liked artistic men, sophisticated *bon vivants* with a penchant for poetry and a flair for tennis.

Roses are red, violets are blue, I can't wait to get a naked view of you, ran through my mind.

"You say something, Harry?"

I shook my head. "Oh, just versifying my thoughts," I replied.

"Um," she said. "The veal chops in orange puree sounds divine."

She did that thing with her tongue again. I noticed the fullness of her mouth. As I watched her listen to the dessert recording, I versified a few more fantasies, all of them involving Adina's mouth.

Oh, ignite my waiting wick; give a kiss to my rising …

"I know I'm going to have the brûlée for dessert," she interrupted my thoughts. "Vanilla and banana, sounds divine, doesn't it?"

Actually, it sounded like sloppy baby food, but instead of simply agreeing, I pretended to salivate.

"What are you doing, Harry?" she asked.

"Foaming at the mouth," I said.

She sat back and raised her eyebrows again, her eyes large and dark. I imagined them under me and foamed at the mouth again.

"Jesus," she said.

"What, you don't say bejesus?" I asked in astonishment.

"There really was a man named Jesus," she said.

"It's old English," I retorted. "Just like Ghoul used to be God."

She looked at me as she would a fly in her soup.

I sat back and coughed. "I'm not usually this inept," I said.

She softened her speech for the first time. "So, tell me, Harry. What are you 'usually' then?"

I coughed again. It was all going to come out. The virtual sex rooms instead of real experience, real women. Usually inept, I thought. I knew I was as red as a fire truck and came off like an inexperienced virgin, even though that was impossible. Boys had to be initiated into sex at the age of twelve. However, after the age of twelve, my experiences came to a screeching halt, except for an occasional bang with someone I managed to pull out of a bar.

"Well, I'm usually quite in control of myself," I said.

Who was I kidding? I was a freak let out of his cage for the night to gross-out a totally beautiful woman.

"You don't seem to have any control at all," she said and laughed. "Perhaps you should join the twelve-step program for geeks … I hear the city universities have a good one."

Right then and there, I wanted a woman who thought I was fascinating and handsome, a brilliant conversationalist, sexiest man alive – I wanted some sweet little perky blonde who came from Kansas and sucked hay and didn't think of me as a geek. Adina Cordova was way over my head and had insulted me to the core. Mother was right.

"You're downright offensive, Harry," she said.

I would delete her first thing in the morning, send off a new profile and wait for a woman who didn't make me sweat.

We ate in near silence, chatting only about the food, which was worth the attention. Maxwell's was one of the only restaurants in New York where steak was still under four hundred bucks a plate.

It was after we finished off a bottle of wine that she took my hand. Perhaps she wouldn't have otherwise.

"So, what do you do for a living, Harry? You've never mentioned."

"I'm a cartoonist," I said.

"Which one?" she asked.

"Reginald Brat, Super Star and … Mandero." I gave her a weak smile. Women never liked Mandero.

As I suspected, she shuddered. "Tough man, that Mandero, but his eyes are cool and his face … so fierce, Harry. Unlike yours." She giggled and I blushed.

"He used to be nice," I offered.

"I think there's more to you than meets the eye, Harry," she said. I felt her palm as it slid over mine. I was aroused simply by her touch. Maybe deleting her was a bit hasty.

"Those imails between us were so sweet. I fell a bit in love with you."

She sounded like an old movie. In love? But I smiled anyway. I think I remembered reading that if you agreed with a woman, they'd take you to bed.

"Me, too," I said sheepishly.

"Will you walk me home?" she said softly, touching the side of my cheek. "I don't live far."

"Not far? Where's that? I mean, really?" I stammered like an idiot.

"You're funny," she said. "And you have lovely eyes."

"Wow," I said, again like an idiot.

She took a final sip of her latte. "You so fit my profile." She gazed at me a little dreamily, I thought. "Except for the poetry, never heard of Millay, have you?"

"Samuel Millay, the guy who invented the non-flush whish toilet? Sure, I have."

"Edna St. Vincent." She sighed. "I guess your Computer Project Education sees no need for poetry?"

"Not beyond third grade," I said, "Nursery rhymes. You had the same education, didn't you?"

"My father had read all of Shakespeare's plays to me by then. He recited Wordsworth, Shelly, Elizabeth Barrett Browning. Daddy loves poetry, too. Of course, we haven't had poetry for nearly thirty years."

"Oh," I said. "I'm afraid I don't know those names at all. The Brain has deemed literature and poetry unnecessary."

She frowned. "I still find you credible, Harry," she said. "I can't wait to read *Lady Chatterley's Lover* to you."

"How's that?" I asked. I sounded more normal than I had all evening.

"You still have a human side, despite your missing education."

"Oh?" I said. I'd never quite thought of myself as being human, as if it meant something other than just being human, not a machine, or whatever. Adina implied that human meant more.

"You're very beautiful," I said. "Grrrrrr."

When she laughed, all heads turned toward us. But, there was something different about her. She laughed without malice.

01001111001101111011000100110111111011001000111100100100110111100110011000000101001001101111011011000010110010

I not only walked her home that evening. I took her to bed. She was so willing to have me in her arms. I socked it to her, if you'll forgive the term; I hadn't yet learned to be poetically literate. She socked it to me in every way I'd imagined … her incredible mouth on my bare skin. Holy George Gordon Lord Byron! That was a poet I learned about that evening.

"'She walks in beauty like the night,'" Adina recited.

I had never heard words more appropriate to my feelings.

"'With cloudless chimes and starry skies. And all that's best of dark and bright. Meet in her aspect and her eyes.'"

"Wow! I'll have more of that, Adina."

"'Which heaven to gaudy day denies.'"

Flying through space, breaking free, merging souls: that was Adina's term; I never would have thought of it. But she was right, it wasn't just sex; it was something beyond the stickiness of our bodies. I couldn't name it but I wanted never to let her go.

"I love you," she said as she kissed my cheek, after hours of sliding over each other like blissful trapeze artists.

The reference to love shocked me: love was in the soul file. "Love? You mean you didn't delete it?" I asked in amazement. "You're serious about it?"

"Of course I'm serious," she said. "You didn't delete your file, did you? I mean, you don't act like a man without a soul file."

Suddenly, I felt heavy, that if I fell, I'd break into a million pieces and she'd gather up all the jagged ends and edges and send them out to sea. I'd exist in a bottle, floating over a wave and I'd never see the shore again.

"No," I said. "I've no file on love. It's from the old days. I mean it's archaic. I'm sorry. How could you have a love file? We're not permitted access to it. You were born here, born to the same rules as I was."

"I was wrong about you, Harry. I misunderstood. You were so gentle and sweet, I thought …"

"Thought what?"

"Nothing, sorry I brought it up. I should have checked … I just assumed."

"Assumed what?"

"Nothing."

I looked away. "I didn't mean to upset you," I said, apologetically. "I just thought we were all the same."

She threw her pillow at the wall and it knocked a few things off the bureau. "I fucked up," she said. "I thought you might have been a member …"

"A member of what?"

"Never mind."

"This doesn't have to end, Adina. The sex was great, didn't you think?"

"Get out, Harry. We have no future. I'm sorry, it will never work between us. What could I possibly have been thinking?"

"No, please, Adina, it doesn't have to end, really it doesn't."

"Don't you get it, Harry?"

I stood there gaping at her, as I had the night before in the bar. "Get what?" I asked.

"You're one of them," she said sadly. "And I am not."

CHAPTER FIVE

I hated the crowded streets, but had no choice other than to walk them. That's just the way it was, crowds everywhere. Always everywhere.

I felt miserable. I didn't know what Adina was talking about when she said I didn't get it, or why the love file would be so damn important to her. By the time I was born, no one was permitted to access the soul file which contained the love file. Not under any circumstances. The Computer Project told us everything in it was just a concept, and if opened, dysfunction would proliferate.

The word 'soul' defined everything that couldn't be proven. God and all religions were included, as was love. Also in the soul file were reincarnation, psychic phenomena, ghosts … things like that. I wanted to read the file word for word now that not having read it had cost me Adina. However, the lack of the soul file didn't make me a freak; it made me rational. Rationality was especially important to the future of Computer Project children. We didn't fall in love, as in days of old. We either fucked or we paired. When we paired, we married. When we fucked, we were lucky. That's the way it was.

I walked into Central Park and took the shortcut, for I had permission to do so. Passes to the park were expensive but the wealthy families on and around Central Park West owned lifelong contracts to access it, one of the privileges of living a block from Central Park, and being wealthy, of course. I used my pass often, though I rarely found solitude there.

Central Park was crowded at night because many people, aside from my family, were granted park privileges. It was dark, nearly pitch black. The city was always dimly lit at night. I walked over a few couples on my way home; relieved I had not stepped on a hand or tripped over a foot. I knew they were engrossed in sex. I'd never had sex in the park, preferring the virtual rooms instead. At least it was private. I was reluctant to fornicate in front of hundreds of others. I guess that's why the few heterosexual women left in the city wouldn't date me, and men called me queer. Be that as it may, rats ran all over the place at night. I couldn't bear fornicating for the pleasure of the rats, or the voyeurs. Personally, I found it disgusting because many computers had cameras on the park and if people tuned in, they could vote for the couple with the best sexual creativity. The show was called *Best in Sex*. I think the winners were given a weekend orgy in the Poconos.

I finally made it home. A few women had tugged at my sleeve and offered me the pleasure of their company, however brief it might be, and I'd refused. These weren't whores out in the night either; they were just poor women who had snuck in and sought sex with the wealthy, hoping to be swept up and placed in one of the apartments on Central Park West. Of course, the poor women were deluded; they were used for pleasure and rejected afterward, but hope springs eternal, I guess, a popular phrase for defining a poor man's plight.

I walked past the doorman, all but weeping like a baby.

If my love file was deleted, why was I suffering?

I sat down on my bed and stared at the computer around me. It blinked at me with maniacal steadiness, overwhelming me with the desire to smash it. I should have stopped off at the Fist In Your Face Club. I could have taken out my aggression there. I didn't know why I was angry, but the emotion might have exploded inside me and left me dead in my room, it was so intense.

Supposed to turn off my computer when I finished using it, I might have been fined if it ever came to the attention of The Brain, but I guess I was so excited to see Adina that I forgot to flip the plug. We were all committed to using electricity sparingly; Mother lit candles after dark, as did restaurants and bars. The only permissible full-wattage low-energy bulbs were in hospitals.

I glanced at my imails. I needed to send a note to Adina and beg her to see me again. I'd tell her I would learn everything she could teach me, everything that The Brain had stolen.

I pointed my finger at 'compose' and poured out my heart. I hit 'send' without rereading it, distressed to see an Error Report come back to me. Adina had already blocked all correspondence from Harry Erin Cooper. I put my head in my hands and wept even more deeply than before. My despair was indescribable. What had she done to me? In my mind, she'd not only deleted me from her computer but off the face of the earth, and I had vanished entirely – my body, my whole being. If I really did have a soul, it was being ripped from me inch by inch, if that's possible.

My father must have heard my sobs, for he stood in my doorway and frowned as if we'd lost our meat ration for the month.

"What is it, son?"

I told him everything. I guess I sought comfort and hoped my father would provide it. I admitted to him how I had made a total ass of myself at dinner with Adina, but she liked me anyway. My father took my hand and squeezed it.

"I was afraid of this," he said.

"She took me to bed, Dad. She not only took me to bed, but to the stars, to somewhere I'd never been before, and that place where she took me rattled me from within."

"Ah, love," I heard my father whisper.

I was startled. "What do you know of it?"

"Plenty," he said.

I was astonished but I didn't question him, too wrapped up in my despair.

"For the first time since my birth, I understood that there's a lightness to life. Will I ever feel that way again?" I asked.

"Happiness," my father whispered. "I see you found happiness tonight."

"Yes," I said and nodded my head. "But I lost it so soon."

Suddenly, he hugged me. I sat silently in his arms for a while before he sat back and spoke. "I was hoping I'd never have to say this, Harry, never have to tell you the truth. I wanted to protect you."

"What truth?"

"Your love file was not deleted. It's safely tucked away in your soul file."

I shot up and stood before him. "What are you saying?"

"I couldn't do it to you. I refused to raise you without a soul, son."

My heart thumped in my chest. "Why the hell didn't you tell me? How could you keep something like that to yourself?"

"Survival, son. Love will weaken you. If The Brain gets wind of it, you'll be taken."

"What, taken where?"

"Everywhere we can't go on our own."

I had no idea what he was talking about, but my head ached listening to him. I took a breath that lasted three minutes.

"What about Mother?" I asked, still shocked at what my father had kept from me. "Does she know that my soul file wasn't deleted?"

"Yes, she knows. Perhaps we should have educated you to it, but we chose not to."

"I don't understand. When the hell were you going to tell me?"

"It's dangerous to know you're different."

I watched my father turn his eyes to the wall, where the computer bleeped, downloaded and updated.

"Here, let me show you something," he said.

He took the keyboard we rarely used and logged back into the site he had shown me earlier, the one that had posted Adina's newsletter. I'm not very technical but my father is. He builds computers from scratch. That's what he does for a living, builds small replicas of The Brain for use outside the home. I watched, absolutely stunned, as he quickly shifted in and out of screens. He moved through codes. Finally, he went through a series of logins, all of them different.

"Where are you?" I asked.

"I want your word."

"About what?"

"No one is to see this site unless they're a member. I intended to show it to you if you ever … fell in love." He looked over at me. "I'm afraid I was hoping you wouldn't. Come here, Harry. I'll show you how to get onto *it*. But you've got to memorize it, write nothing down. Promise?"

"I promise, Father."

"It's called *Âme*."

"*Âme*?"

"French for psyche. It's a site that originated in France. Now it's available to all its members, all over the world.

You've always had a password."

"Why aren't we living in France then?"

"Try to go abroad and see what happens. You'll lose all privileges, and your passport will be deleted for all time. The Cordovas were responsible for an underground movement that's keeping the arts alive in Europe. It's far worse here, Harry, we have nothing. There is no underground in America, except for the Classes in Courage."

I looked at him helplessly. None of it made sense. But then again, we knew only what we were allowed to know. "'Classes in Courage?'" I asked.

"They're taught all over the world. The Cordovas had a lot to do with rounding up teachers and starting up the classes. Then the government authorities of each country wanted to get rid of Cordova and The Brain knew he was a troublemaker and a loudmouth. I don't know how he managed to survive. Of course, the family was deported for opening their big mouths and protesting. They were lucky they weren't killed. But, I guess, no one gets rid of a good chef." He chuckled. "Not even The Brain."

"I don't believe this."

"*Âme* is a secret underground of people who believe in the concept of soul, individualism, prophets like Jesus, or to put it simply, freedom of thought, freedom of speech. The site is coded not to bring up any alerts to The Brain."

"I don't believe this," I said again as I stood behind him and watched. He brought up a list of names. "What's that?"

"They are all members of *Âme*."

"And our names are there?"

He nodded. "We're listed so we can find each other, but no one must find us. You'll memorize the codes and logins but never write them down. Access to it is limited, probably why Adina didn't check to see if you were on it."

"Well, I see she would have found me."

"No doubt."

46

"Why did you feel it necessary to create a site like this?"

"Because we believe that everything in the soul file is subject to choice. But we must use the file sparingly to avoid capture. We also believe that humanity is being destroyed by the originators of The Brain, who have no real thought, just mindless desire, mindless greed. You might say they're creating dead people with a heartbeat. Soon, Harry, The Brain will annihilate humanity, as we know it. God knows what will walk the earth. We're trying to stop it, however we can."

"What are you saying, The Brain is going to destroy us?"

"In many ways, It already has."

What he was saying was true, but I couldn't articulate how I knew it.

"We're being eaten, Harry. Everything beautiful has been taken from us. We're robots on the earth paying credence to a leader we've never seen. Even melody is gone. You don't know music at all, you know."

"Of course, I do. I know music," I said. Music was what we moved our bodies to, a sexual call to copulation, anger and lust. Sometimes we warmed up to it at the Fist in Your Face Club.

"No, you don't know music, you know sound. You know a clash of cymbals and drums. Some temper tantrum on a piano, the rape of a guitar, angry wails, that's what you know. Hear, listen to this." He went to his download file and double-clicked on something called Mozart.

The volume was low, but I heard it. "Wow," I said. "It's strange."

"How about this," he said.

My father and I listened for about a half-hour to music by the Beatles, Simon and Garfunkel and Cole Porter.

"This was once considered music, Harry."

I'd heard old music before but nothing like that. Sometimes we'd get out this stuff from the early century and

47

play it while we were shooting rats. They used to call all of it heavy metal or rap, but in my day, we just called it Rat Kill.

"Hope, love, passion have been dismissed, son. We exist to feed The Brain, and only that. How many hours a day do we work and how many drugs do we take to do it? How many hours do we sleep, four? There's no life for us, there's just subservience."

"I don't understand."

My father laughed. "Our souls have died, Harry. Some of us fight to keep just a flicker of humanity alive."

"Humanity? That's a term. You say it as if it's more than that, like Adina did tonight. I still don't understand."

"You will." He typed in something I couldn't see. "There you are, Harry, all your files."

I looked at what must have been hundreds of files. Love was at the top.

"Why didn't you tell me?"

"Sensitivity is dangerous. If we allowed you to become sensitive, we'd put you at risk. I promised your mother that I would never give you the file. When you said Adina's name, we surmised immediately that her father educated her on the soul file. As I said, Cordova is a very unusual man. We knew if you fell under Adina's influence you'd start to feel, to wonder, to hope. Perhaps, even to rebel."

If I'd had wings, I'd have flown at that moment, even though Adina had deleted me from her Moon list where I had surely existed as a contact, I was sure I could reach her by instant communication blue speed, she'd have to turn it back on at some point. I would let her know I had everything needed to claim her as my bride.

"You have a lot of reading to catch up on, Harry," my father said to me.

"I can't wait," I responded.

"What is your young woman's name again?"

"Adina," I said and watched as father looked up her file.

"She's here," he said, "Along with her whole family. They're blacklisted, of course. They won't ever be able to reenter Italy now that they've returned to the US. The Brain doesn't allow any trips abroad anymore anyway. If Cordova managed to slip out years ago, it's a wonder they didn't kill him on the way back in, especially as he's an insurgent. He bribed someone, I'm sure of it. Must have saved his life."

"Bribed?" I was confused. "How does one bribe The Brain?"

"He's a chef. Whoever sits behind the computer eats. I would imagine." He chuckled.

"What does that mean? We're all held prisoner?"

"The Brain thinks we are all in acceptance of the world it has created, but clearly, we are not all so misguided. Listen, son, news sites tell us all the time that we don't have the fuel for transatlantic flights and only certain people can fly, like government officials. That's not true. No one flies. And there aren't any government officials. There's a wall around this country, Harry and it's too high to jump, too strong to tear down."

"Oh," I said.

Father turned off the computer. "Don't you see, Harry?" he said.

"See what?"

"The world around you is run by a computer. The man or men who sit behind its keys cannot be destroyed in today's world or by today's weapons. Our president is a digital image. Our news is fiction. Eventually, our technology consumed us, quietly and viciously. There is no real flesh and blood anymore. Oh, people still have heartbeats, but they're empty vessels, they serve The Brain, nothing else. In our world, the robots have equal footing, loaded with brains that function like ours, but without a soul, and you can't distinguish the difference unless you fall in love, nor can you still find people with a human soul. The precious few."

I sat back with a thud. All my life I'd felt it, the unnaturalness, the indifference. What had the Computer Project really done to us? I wanted to speak to my father more, but I fell asleep. I simply passed out. I must have been exhausted.

I dreamed that night that I flew through Adina's window. I dreamed I carried her off to a place very much like a fairy tale, where music was soft like the sounds my father had played me, and the wind carried echoes – melodic, boundless, and euphonious.

CHAPTER SIX

Adina

have only six children this year. That is good, much more manageable. If there is damage, perhaps I can see it immediately and work more closely with the afflicted child.

The children have come to us through *Âme*. They are lucky to have parents who refuse to delete their soul files. Memory loss is more and more prevalent each year, so every member of *Âme* is nervous. We're aware of the rise in murders committed by children, so we try to speed up our efforts, but we're far outnumbered. We persevere, despite that. Across the country, there are factions, small classes like mine, in which we try to eradicate the damages of Computer Project educations and silently build our own army. If our children grow up to care enough about future generations, they will destroy The Brain. That destruction is our purpose.

Our psychiatrists have told us, in various reports, that as children lose their memories, they no longer bond, nor do they feel anything for anyone outside of themselves, and what serves them. Presented to The Brain, these noted psychiatric reports were, of course, all called insubstantial and ignored.

As a journalist, I often write about the effects of Computer Education on developing minds, but all of my articles are pulled. The emotional damage is unimaginable, a result of deplorable indifference and isolation. In the Computer Project, each child is educated in a cubbyhole. The cubbyhole contains a computer and nothing else. During recesses, children can watch films produced by The Brain, a total bunch of propaganda that further anesthetizes them to emotion, desire and compassion.

All Computer Project children are closely monitored until they turn eighteen. From an early age, they're given endless tests, and educational emphasis is then placed upon individual abilities until a particular vocation is chosen for them. From that point, the children focus on learning their trades and professions. Some will go on to college, but all will work for The Brain exclusively after they graduate. College is simply preparation for employment by The Brain. Private enterprises are Brain-controlled. Businesses believed to be individually owned are not, they are all subject to The Brain's codes of conduct, taxes and laws. In essence, nobody owns anything but The Brain.

Nothing in a Computer Project Education is funny, sad or enlightening. As a result, the children feel estranged and disassociated. They can only remember what The Brain deems necessary for survival. They feel angry, frustrated and alone. If they reach maturity, they can survive. If they bring harm to one another, or to their parents, they are regarded as undesirable and imprisoned, or in some cases, shot.

I attribute the entire atrocity of our society to The Brain, and the psychopaths it creates, through Computer Project educations. Like the rest of us, the children are sleep deprived from an early age, making them further vulnerable to The Brain's control. They are also drugged, practically from the moment they're born, inhibiting growth and further damaging their minds. Naturally, imagination is not encouraged, unless it serves a purpose, like Harry's comic heroes, created to offer violence to a generation that craves it, that needs the expression of violence for the release of energy, and any residue of pent-up emotions. Children are impressionable and easily destroyed by the lack of love and nurturing they should have received, had they available parents.

Âme is a covert society and will never outnumber The Brain's army of drones, soulless aberrations bred to feed The Brain's greed, The Brain's directives, agendas and thirst for power. But if enough children are saved, I believe they'll outsmart this atrocity, and it will finally collapse in on itself.

I don't know where it's all headed; I can only do my part and pray for a miracle, for some divine intervention. So, for the last three years, I have held classes in my parent's apartment. Computer Project educations are given for the entire day, but we have found a way to appear logged on, and we steal the time back, usually, in the early mornings. If I am discovered teaching the soul file to children, my family and I will be killed. I don't know what the enemy looks like, so I'd be easy to annihilate. However, if I don't teach these children, they will evolve into killers, predators and madmen, and The Brain will continue to thrive.

So far, I have had success. My students appear to be thinking and feeling human beings. They show normal emotions for their age, for the most part. If we can educate enough of them, perhaps we can restore the world to the way it was prior to the mistakes made after the nineteenth century. A crystal ball would have come in handy then.

If our ancestors had only known that the advancement of technology and the wrong people in power would create Computer Project educations and babies would be robbed of their souls, they might have taken notice of the malignancy and curtailed it. If they only knew that future generations would grow up to become so much like animated machines, future generations that would accept the darkness and know nothing else but the emptiness.

Each new baby born has the potential to become more violent, more damaged by the Computer Project, unless there are enough of us to intervene. In a city of millions, I have only six. But there are thousands like me.

Sometimes, I do feel hopeless, but if I can save just one child, well, then, I have made a difference; I've taken a strike against The Brain. I've tried to educate the children with the spirituality they lack by instilling in their selfish egos that they are not everything, or the center of existence. Maybe there is a God and maybe he has left it up to us to find him. Maybe The Brain is nothing more than the result of past indifference. Maybe by believing more in one, we destroy the other.

Life is not the glorious experience it once was, the world I have read about before the world imploded. It is bleak, hopeless, isolated and selfishly one-dimensional. But The Brain has a purpose, I imagine, or perhaps not. Perhaps it exists at random, created subversively while no one was looking.

This year Edward is my favorite student, though I love them all. Edward is gifted at the piano. I love to discover creative ability in children. Pianos are difficult to get hold of, but my father has had one moved from a museum in South Carolina. They had to gut an old theater because of a fire but the piano was saved. It cost Daddy five steaks, but it was worth it. Now Edward can play to his heart's content. My mother has taught him to read music and he has learned to compose. What can I do with him in a world that only knows noise and violently graphic lyrics? Where can I send him with his brilliant gift but to France? In the arms of *Âme* he will flourish. There is an underground there, it is almost like a new country, but he will have to be subversively snuck into the country and that will not be easy.

In my parent's house, there is a secret room. Behind the door is where Edward plays. On the walls are books, copies of manuscripts, sheet music and old CDs. As the sun comes in and throws its patterns on the walls, the children sit and listen to me as I teach. They anticipate the knowledge of a world they are not familiar with. I open the soul file for them. I don't teach religion, but I tell them what it is. I don't sanction the paranormal, but I debate with them the possibility. I recite poetry and they learn to love language. When they weep, I am overjoyed.

There is no computer in our secret room. As a matter of fact, only an old CD player is allowed, and occasionally, a television for films. The children are not permitted to imail; they write in longhand. They are not to bastardize the language with abbreviations, and they cannot use sentences, whether spoken or written, that are not grammatically correct.

Omiyinka, one of the twins, is from an African-American family. I am told her grandfather was a senator in the United States government in the old America. He died several years ago. I believe he was killed for opposing the closing of schools for wealthy children with the replacement of Computer Project educations. How did we let it happen, you might ask? It resulted from apathy, workplace takeovers, and the one-hundred-year or so decline of conventional education. Many think The Brain is a corporation that grew into a monster and swallowed us while our backs were turned.

When Omiyinka first came to me, she was furious because I banned any use of Mighty Me iPods while out in public – no texting, no talking, no music. Rudeness was a subject I taught last year. Omiyinka wound up with an A. Her sister, Michelle, had a harder time adjusting to the concept of brotherly love, compassion, and community service.

I found that one of the best ways to teach humanity was to show films that depicted the lack of it. They understood then that emotional pain is preventable. When we bring it upon each other, it's deplorable. But emotional pain is necessary. If we don't mourn, we don't love. I try to teach them that we are all part of a greater whole. If that whole is sick, we will eventually all die from the same disease.

The children and I debate the subject of death often. My youngest student, Sam, believes in heaven. We don't dissect Sam's belief or ask him to prove that heaven exists. We honor his conclusions and allow him to express them. We question the existence of God without interpretation or answers. Questions get us to think, answers close our minds. That is precisely what The Brain does to us: it answers all our questions with its own deafening lie.

As a journalist, I can steal hours from The Brain that most people can't. Unfortunately, I cannot escape the drugs I must take to exist, to get through the day. Many of the drugs cause side effects, most of which are curable, so it has become a vicious circle; each drug needs a drug that needs another drug.

We let others use the secret room to keep the children's souls alive, as well. They, too, can steal time. Some of them teach in the institutions, sell products and services in the field, and even fix Zippies. Luckily, The Brain has not discovered the existence of what we have come to call "classes in courage."

All the children in my class this year can memorize, which was a dying art by the twenty-first century. The children can solve math problems, remember historic dates, and the names of presidents, except for Bertram. He worries me the most. His Computer Education has been instilled in his brain and he is the oldest. When I asked him the name of his dog yesterday, he couldn't recall. It is this lack of memory that creates this breed of monsters. I'm trying to save him, to help him establish bonds, learn to think on his own but he grows increasingly distant.

Little Sara clings to me constantly and it breaks my heart. Servants and robots are raising Sara. Her ninety-year-old grandmother brought her to me last year and begged me to teach her. Since no child is refused, I accepted Sara, even knowing she was suffering emotionally and severely damaged. Her grandmother has been farmed out to a home for the aged, where most people over the age of seventy are sent. Sara's parents are Computer Project children and see nothing wrong with their daughter. Mrs. Cromwell, Sara's grandmother, who can no longer teach her, is trying to save the girl; Mrs. Cromwell has been reduced to an angry, frightened, frustrated old woman by a society that detests the old, seeing in them their own fears about the natural process of aging. Fortunately, the old are not monitored and she was able to bring Sara to me.

"Please help her," Mrs. Cromwell begged. "Please."

But Sara is so frightened by the world around her that she barely speaks. I've been teaching her now for five months. I have recently noticed her crush on Edward, though. I can only hope she will trust him enough to, at least, sit beside him.

Teaching the children has been my life since I graduated college. I don't think of men very much. In my world, most of them are deplorable. Harry was a sweet surprise. I can't say he was a disappointment at all. I never expected any miracles. I continue to think of him, and I know I could love him. But I will not let myself weaken to his charm. He has not been enlightened and it scares me to love a man who is more attuned to his libido than any capacity to feel a human emotion, or to sustain one. I have deleted his name from my Moon list and hope he'll accept the rejection. It has been three weeks and so far, he has not banged down my door, a good sign.

Today is a strange day. Harry is not the only man who scares me. I received a ping from a man named Crater. He pinged me early, after first contacting me by imail. He insisted I meet him tonight at Maxwell's. I sensed a threatening intensity to his tone that I didn't like but he mentioned having answers I might find valuable. I immediately pinged my father, who said I should go, and he would not be far, just in case.

"I have a feeling about this," Daddy said. "Call it intuition. This Crater calls out of the blue? Does he know something about the Classes in Courage?"

"God, I hope not."

"He may try to blackmail you."

"You think this is important?" I wasn't sure. "Maybe I should ignore it."

"Could be the most important dinner date you've ever had. I need to mediate. This is all ringing a bell. The name is familiar to me."

I sighed. Daddy thought he was a clairvoyant.

"What'd he say exactly?" Daddy asked.

"'It's all going to fall apart,'" I said. "Maybe you need to print that."

"You're kidding? Those were his words?"

"Yes, I'm quoting what he said."

"Anything else?"

"Yes, he said 'I have a crystal ball that says America is in for financial disaster and the little prick behind it needs to die.'"

"So he believes in crystal balls?"

"Maybe."

"Well, you're a journalist. How can you refuse?"

And so, I pinged him back and said I'd be there.

CHAPTER SEVEN

Adina would not see me, nor would she take my calls, and of course, I was blocked from her imail. I decided the only way to contact her was to show up at Maxwell's. She liked the place and would probably be there on Saturday night. I hoped she had the same time off that I did.

As it turned out, it was three whole Saturdays before I found her at Maxwell's. When I finally did, she wasn't alone. She was sitting at a table having dinner with three other people. From where I stood, it looked like a double date. I gulped and went back to the bar. Did I really want to do this, make a complete fool of myself again?

After a scotch and water, I gathered my nerve and approached her table only to be shocked. Even more, repulsed. She was sitting with a man who looked like a snake. Pencil thin, his hair was greased and spiked at the top of his head. Dark slits for eyes and leathery, wrinkled skin added to his repellant appearance. I swear I saw fangs at the side of his mouth, but to my amazement, the fangs were rings pierced into his lip. His knuckles looked deformed and popped off his hands like small rocks.

As I took him in more closely, I gasped. He was an

android. I could tell by the way he moved. Our society has many of them. This one, it appeared, was rather old and may even have been created in the early twentieth century. They were usually strictly for amusement then, like pets.

"Harry, what are you doing here?" Adina asked as she looked up at me.

I stood tongue-tied. I couldn't begin to imagine why Adina would have any interest at all in this caricature of a human being. Not in my wildest imagination could I have conceived of him and I'm one hell of a good cartoonist.

"Hi, Adina," I said and stood firm, eyeing the other two cretins at the table. They were just as weird. I surmised they were also androids, human-looking robots, though just barely.

"How are you, Harry?" Adina smiled politely, but if I had to guess her temperature, I would compare it to what used to be a January winter.

"Fine," I said.

I think she was waiting for me to leave. Instead, I held my hand out to the android next to her. He took my hand in his and startled me with how human it felt.

"Oh, this is Harry, Crater. Crater, Harry," Adina said, still as cool as a meat-packing plant.

He gave me what would have been a cold, damp shake, had he any blood in his veins. I couldn't believe his name. We'd all gone back to normal names years ago, right after Jim, Joan and Joe became exotic. What parent would name their child Crater? Yes, these androids had parents. They even had thought processes, but they weren't real. They doubled as waiters, taxi drivers, even actors when needed. They cleaned our houses and excelled in math, that's why so many were in charge of corporations. They all worked for The Brain.

"Pleased to meet you," Crater mumbled as he stared at me.

"Oh, and this is Bridge and her brother, Tunnel." Adina had spoken the introductions quickly, rather dismissively, I thought.

I wanted to laugh but didn't. Bridge wore a ton of makeup: green eyebrows and purple lips, created that way, I assume. Quite an ugly android. Her hair. too, was spiked and stood up in orange twigs. Her top lip was full of jewelry and tattoos covered her shoulders. But as an android, she was a work of art. Her skin was the same as real skin, or should I say human skin.

"Hello, hero," she said. "Back atcha."

Before I could decipher her greeting, Tunnel reached over and took my hand. "Hello, stud," he said.

He was huge. He made three or four Craters. He wore a slimy-colored suit, his nails polished blue. He was bald as a newborn and had a tattoo of Galactica on his forehead.

"So, you're our papa?" Tunnel said as he stood up, his legs like tree trunks, and circled me. To my amazement Crater joined him. "The infamous creator of Bridge and Tunnel?" He looked at Crater and grinned.

"I didn't know I was infamous." I glared at him, and chose to ignore Crater, whose aftershave lotion made me sneeze.

"Sensitive," Tunnel said to Crater as he sat back down. Crater stayed upright, staring at my face.

"Amazing," he said.

Adina was as startled by their behavior as I was. Yet she didn't look at me.

I smiled at Bridge but made no motion to leave, aware Adina was terribly uncomfortable.

"Do you mind?" I said to Crater as he stuck his face so close to mine, his lip jewelry could have bruised me.

He laughed at me and slunk back to his seat.

"Do you need me?" I asked Adina.

She cocked her head to one side. "What are you talking

about, Harry? Why would I need you?"

"Well, it looks to me like you're being held captive by three of the ugliest androids I've ever seen in my life."

Crater and Tunnel rose from the table at the same time. I stood my ground, even though Tunnel could have broken my neck with one hand. Bridge laughed in high-pitched squeals.

"For God's sake, Harry, you're being rude," Adina said, looking ravishing, wrapped in a dress with no back and not much of a front. Despite the threat to my last breath, I devoured the vision with my eyes.

"I need to speak to you," I said.

Angry, all I thought of at that point was knocking Crater to the ground; Tunnel would have been more difficult. I gritted my teeth at Tunnel instead and snarled in his face He looked back at mine and spat. There's no winning with a robot and I knew it.

"That took a lot of talent," I said, wiping his slime from my face.

Adina had looked away. She appeared furious, but I was also angry, so much so, I wanted to pound on the table.

"I would like to speak with you, Adina," I repeated.

"I'm busy, Harry." She glared at me. "I'm on assignment."

A woman tried to squeeze past me at that point as I blocked the narrow passage between chairs. On impulse, I grabbed the poor woman and kissed her. That would show Adina I'm not a man to be cheated on.

I heard Adina say "asshole" as my tongue slipped over the skinny blonde's lips, her breasts bore into my chest, and my erection popped through my fly. The tension around me worked very much like Viagra.

After much grinding of bodies, the blonde finally broke my hold and smiled at me. "Good to meet you too," she said. "Want to find a corner?"

I looked over at Adina. Rockets seemed to fly from her

eyes. "You're an idiot," she said.

I fumed for a few seconds more, a time bomb about to blow, before leaving Maxwell's. The skinny blonde didn't leave with me, but followed me to the exit.

"Leaving so soon?" she asked.

"You won't be alone long," I said to her and slammed the door behind me.

01.001.11.001.1.011.111.011.0001.001.1.011.111.011.1.001.0001.111.001.001.11.011.1.1001.1.001.000001.01.001.001.101.111.011.0001.01.1.001.00

I got to the Fist in Your Face Club a few minutes later and assaulted a guy who danced around like a frigging penguin. He yelped when he took my punches, which startled me, and then I realized he did that to throw me off guard. I beat the shit out of him anyway and left feeling tired. I could have sunk into a river, if we had any, which we didn't.

01.001.11.001.1.011.111.011.0001.001.1.011.111.011.1.001.0001.111.001.001.11.011.1.1001.1.001.000001.01.001.001.101.111.011.0001.01.1.001.00

I showed up at Adina's apartment the next morning, praying I wouldn't find Tunnel next to a cup of coffee and a condom. I hear androids can have sex and some people buy them just for that purpose, rather than deal with real men or women.

"You're having an affair with that android, Tunnel?" I asked as she stood aside to let me in.

"I don't remember inviting you for breakfast, Harry."

"Is he here?"

She stared at me so hard I thought I might have forgotten to dress. "What are you going to do, Harry, pull the wires out of his body?"

"Is he here?" I asked again, with a great deal more fervor.

"No," she said. "What about the blonde?"

I might have burst out crying, but instead, I sat at the kitchen bar and breathed a sigh of relief.

"Look," I said slowly. "Forget the blonde, I did that to

hurt you. I ditched her at the door."

"Don't do that again, Harry, it was crass … you had an erection."

"Forget the erection. I love you."

She sat close to me. "You're full of surprises."

"You're not dating that asshole, are you? I hear some women like androids."

"My father was at the next table, watching out for me. You're lucky he didn't toss you across the room."

"Your father?" I instinctively straightened my tie.

"Don't worry, no one at Maxwell's acts normal. He probably just thought you were one of the usual jerks."

I smiled, even though I'd just been insulted.

"*Âme.*" I tossed the name at her, so proud of myself I might have burst.

Her eyes widened. I wanted to dive into them and swim to her heart, and sleep beside her ample bosom for the rest of my life.

"How do you know about *Âme*?"

"My father is a member. Mother too. I've got a password, so I guess I'm a member as well, but they didn't want to tell me. I may never forgive them for that. It might have cost me you."

"I know why they didn't want to tell you."

"Why?"

"Harry," she said. "We're living in darkness. All we do is work for The Brain's pleasure. We have no life but the minutes we find in places like Maxwell's, where we search for something that's been missing for so long, we don't even know what it is anymore. Your father didn't want you to ache for it."

"I have been feeling that way, Adina. I really have, that I'm aching."

Then she said something that stunned me.

"Our children are being destroyed. You don't know that,

64

do you? Every generation, it gets worse and there are more and more of them ... these killers."

"Killers? What are you saying?"

"Most of our species are extinct. Most of our rivers have dried. Our air is polluted, our vegetation has rotted and many of our insects and animals are dying. The environment and the despair, or maybe, it's mostly the despair that is causing our children's memory to lapse. It's like Alzheimer's in reverse. Our world is dying, Harry."

"What?"

"Do you have any idea what's happening, or are your parents protecting you from the truth?

"What truth?"

"Murder."

Stunned, discombobulated, horrified. "Murder? We don't murder anymore."

"The Brain controls the news you receive. There are hundreds of murders a day and children commit most of them. They don't remember being nurtured and loved. They don't read. They don't form bonds. What they want, they take. They care nothing for authority. If something gets in their way, they murder it. I'm not allowed to report the news as it is, so no one knows."

"I don't believe this." I almost sank to my knees. "You're a journalist, you have to report it."

"I can't."

"I don't understand."

"Instant deletion. I'd have to learn a different language and everyone else would have to know how to read it. I'd have to report it in a code. I'd have to do what they've done to us, hide the truth behind bullshit. And who's the enemy? Who the fuck is The Brain anyway?"

I put my hands to my face and smothered the impulse to puke.

"Nothing typed into a computer goes unread by The

Brain. I am particularly edited, so I must be careful of what I say. If I were to write that just yesterday, a young boy murdered his mother and then hung himself, it would immediately be deleted."

"Tell me that didn't really happen."

"I can't tell you that."

I remained silent for a long time, my mind in overdrive, confused, my thoughts like avalanches.

"My work is edited too. I haven't thought too much about it until now. Political comment is a joke. My cartoons are more like second-grade humor when I keep it clean. Stupid fornicating caricatures when I go dirty."

"Your parents read my articles, but they probably don't believe me. Or maybe that's what they were protecting you from. Many members of *Âme* can't deal with it. But it's true, Harry. Our children are our enemies unless we can save them."

I got up and went to her. I put my arms around her. "Who is Crater?" I asked. "What the hell were you doing with an android?"

"I got a message on my computer from someone named 'Crater' that said he had information for me, a tip of some kind … something about a prophecy. I didn't know he was an android until I saw him at Maxwell's."

"A prophecy?" I asked.

"Yes, something is supposed to happen that will accelerate what already has happened. Crater called and asked me to meet him at Maxwell's."

"And he showed up with Bridge and Tunnel?"

"Yes, I'd never seen them before, but I knew the minute I did, they were strange. They were all very strange. Usually, androids are insignificant."

"What was the prophecy?" I asked.

"The destruction of the financial markets. Crater told me that someone from the past will destroy the future and I must prevent it. He said even though we'd rebound, to some extent, life would change for the worse and we'd go into a period of darkness and death. He wanted me to expose it. I said it would be deleted. He said we had to find a way to let The Brain know, so he could imprison or kill the person responsible for destroying society. I said I couldn't get information like that to The Brain without being deleted myself."

"Was he satisfied with your answer?"

"I doubt it. I'm sure he wanted me to say I'd do everything I could to get the news to The Brain, but I can't print hearsay like that. I can't trust an android robot. Who's behind him? I mean, they came out of nowhere. It's not credible information, not worth printing. Besides, The Brain would only laugh at prophecy. I told him that."

"How bizarre."

"Anyway, they all left shortly after you did. Before leaving, they told me they were doing me a favor, warning me of harsh retaliation. But it was as if they were more interested in you than in me. Once you left, they were out of there. Did they follow you?"

Without warning, I was adrift, as if I'd fallen off a cliff. Something I'd never experienced before washed over me: unbearable loneliness.

"If I can't be with you, Adina," I said. "I'll become a part of the darkness. I'll never see light again. I need you. Especially after hearing about the children. I can't survive this world without you. It's all too bleak without you."

"Oh, Harry," she said and put her lips to mine. "The only way I can stand living in this world is living with you in it."

"Darling," I whispered, like one of those old movies where people fell in love and called each other "darling." Studying movies in college was compulsory, to analyze the defective behaviors of an earlier society. Suddenly, I wished my blood were celluloid, my heartbeat, a poetic cadence.

I got to my knees. "Will you marry me?"

"Yes," she said as she caressed me. "You're the only man for me, Harry."

"Something to be said for old movies," I whispered.

"What?" she asked as she kissed me again.

"Love isn't altogether fiction, is it?" I asked as I slipped her robe to the floor.

CHAPTER EIGHT

I had lived in ignorance, but it had not been blissful. Like everyone in the world around me, I accepted despair. But then, I met Adina. Happiness shows up sometimes like a penny on the street. Adina told me that if I find a penny on the street with the tail side up, it's lucky. I'd never heard that before; superstition had always been prohibited. But now, I knew I had luck. I had Adina. In the darkness, light glowed, and the tail side was mine.

We had a happy wedding. Everyone was joyful except for Adina's father. He didn't like me. I think he disliked me because I was a cartoonist, and despite my family's affiliation with Âme, he intimated I was superficial, not worthy of his daughter's intelligence.

Well, I can't say I blame him for that. I found reading the soul file tedious. I wanted to talk about what I'd read but I couldn't get a handle on most of it. It took me time to go through the file; I spent hours going over the details, trying to learn the possibilities of an earlier age when people went to churches and temples and had their futures read by gypsies and their dead relatives conjured up by mediums. Reading about the Bible was fun. People lived for hundreds of years and killed each other off like wayward gangsters. It's interesting how we're beginning to live forever, like in the Bible. Since everything is mostly curable, the average life span is one hundred and twenty years. And God really is like The Brain in the Bible, punishing everyone.

"The story about the ark would make a great cartoon," I foolishly said to Adina. She frowned at me and told me not to be so literal when I read it.

"Well, we live to be over a hundred and that was unheard of only a few years ago. It could be true."

"Do you think the Bible was written by people who are from the future, not the past?" she asked me.

Well, that was food for thought but made no sense to me. My wife continued.

"Jesus actually had so little to say, but he became an icon for centuries. Some people, I'm told, still believe him to be the son of God."

"That's irrational," I said.

"What's irrational about it, Harry?"

"We can't prove there is a God or ever was, so how could he have a son? You need flesh and blood to have a son."

"Could you ever believe in something you can't see?"

I thought for a moment. "No, I can only believe in what I see with my own eyes."

"Have you ever seen The Brain?"

"No one has," I said.

"But yet you believed everything it told you."

"No, I didn't."

"What didn't you believe, for instance?" she asked.

"Well, I never believed in cloning. Life should be a spontaneous occurrence. Half the population has cloned itself."

She came over and kissed me. "I'm proud of you for trying to understand, at least."

"Understand what?"

"That we are living in someone else's disbelief."

01.001111001.1011111011.10001.0011.1011111.011.1001.0001.1111001.001.001.11.011.11001.1.001.0000001.01.001.1001.1011.11.011.10001101.1001.00

I was making progress on the soul file and Adina appreciated the attempt, though in all honesty, the only worthy concept in the soul file was love. I knew that to be true because it filled me like warm soup: joy, lightness of being, hope, sweetness, all of it touched me to my soul. If, in fact, I have one.

But no matter how much progress I made in the soul file, it was not appreciated by everyone. No matter how much I loved his daughter, Steven Cordova would never accept me, even if I became an expert on metaphysics. I'm sure he would have preferred that Adina married a subversive babbling poet, someone raised completely removed from any association to The Brain. Steven hated the Computer Project even more than my father. I knew that because of his constant remarks about my generational egoism, my limited knowledge of philosophy and the damage done to me by my Computer Project Education.

I guess I did little to turn the tables and win him over. I, too, detested the devastation of freedom by Computer Project educations. But I loved his daughter deeply, despite my shortcomings, and he should have been grateful for that. It was obvious he considered I'd been damaged by The Brain and was probably a latent serial killer. I must admit, I didn't exactly make the best impression on him when we were together; something about the man brought out an ugly side of me. The very first time we shook hands, I set a precedent for cockfighting.

I had this fantasy before I met Steven Cordova that he would be exactly like my own father, distracted by present politics and relieved to have married off a child. I had expected him to embrace me as my own mother and father had, however reluctantly, embraced Adina. But no, not

Steven Cordova; he was a wild card.

The first day I met Steven, I had also just moved into Adina's apartment. We were to be married in less than two months, and happy to get a jump-start on setting up house together.

Adina lived not far from her parents in Manhattan. While at Columbia, she was allowed to rent one of the larger apartments because she was first on the lease and agreed to roommates. After the roommates moved out, she could keep the apartment if she agreed to marry. The Brain didn't care when she married but insisted on the commitment that someday she would. As a single woman, remaining at college housing would have been her only option, aside from returning home, a move she clearly did not want to make.

I had never requested my own dwelling because my parent's apartment was so large. I had never felt a need to move on, but I did not want to move Adina in. Despite Mother's good intentions, I knew she and Adina would eventually lock horns. Then, of course, there was the problem of fornication. Mother thought nothing of checking in on me as I slept. I did not look forward to Mother's shock when she discovered we slept in the nude, and enjoyed copulating to rat-kill music.

Adina was eventually allowed to purchase her apartment, but if she ever wanted to sell it, it would be difficult. Marriage was an appropriate excuse to sell but it was often difficult to get the sale approved. I feared the worst. Anxious that we might be forced into keeping her apartment after we married, because it would probably be considered large enough for a family, I feared The Brain would deny our request based on a lack of need. This did not please me, for I found her apartment boxy. The bedroom windows faced walls and the kitchen was a long narrow passage with little counter space for a connoisseur cook like me.

Adina and I had argued about how extensively we'd renovate if The Brain denied our request for new housing. I wanted to knock down the wall between the dining room and the kitchen. Dining rooms were so obsolete. No one ate together anymore, anyway. We worked till nine or ten, even longer. Dining rooms might come in handy on Praise The Brain day or Thanksgiving, one of the few remaining holidays we still celebrated, along with July 4th and Labor Day. But other than rare holiday dinners, I saw little use for them. But Adina refused to get rid of the dining room and called me a caveman.

"What about my one hundred Alclad pots?" I shouted. "We need to expand the kitchen."

"Stack them on a shelf, Harry."

"What about my knives, my mixers? You have no place for me to store them."

"Hide them away in a closet."

"That's impractical. I need my appliances at hand."

"When wil you ever have time to cook, Harry?"

"We must make our time, Adina," I said.

01.001.11.001.1.01.1.1.01.1.0001.001.1.01.1.1.1.01.1.001.0001.1.1.1.001.001.001.1.1.01.1.001.1.001.0000001.01.001.001.1.01.1.1.1.01.1.0001.01.1.001.00

And so the argument went, right up to the moment Adina led me into the residence of Steven and Julia Cordova for the first time. We'd walked the short distance, still arguing over the irrationality of storing my whisks in a shoebox.

"You talk some sense into him, Daddy," she said as she let the door slam behind her, nearly catching a few of my fingers and disfiguring me for life. "He sees no use for formal dining."

"So you're a cook?" Steven said to me as I peeked in from behind the door she'd hit me with, rubbing my hand and looking absolutely pathetic. So much for first impressions.

"It's become a hobby," I said. "We have so little time to

practice our culinary skills, but I've developed a passion for it."

Somewhat overbearing, Steven did his best to tower over me like a high rise. He wasn't large like my father, but he was tall and broad-shouldered. His hair was dark, like Adina's. She clearly took after him because his features were very petite, like his nose and his lips, but his eyes were huge; if you can imagine a hawk with grey-green eyes, you'd be looking at Steven. He was well-dressed. Well-dressed men always unsettle me, for I don't have the patience for clothing myself in designer suits and shoes, prissy and expensive waste of time. But on that day, I had worn my best duds, a fancy dark blue tailored pair of slacks, with neat creases, a clean shirt and my brand new classic tassel loafers.

"But it's only a hobby," I said and shook his hand. "Not like you, sir."

"How's your food ration?"

"I cook well with what they give me."

"Takes creative planning."

"Yes, sir, that it does."

"Cooking is a hobby of mine, too."

I was surprised because Steven was a professional chef. "A hobby, sir?"

"I'm retired." He looked at me carefully. "What's your specialty?"

"Beef Wellington. That's something I do quite well."

"Oh, that's so interesting, me too. I'm known as the Welder of Wellington, the Bard of Beef … the Shakespeare of culinary arts. How do you make it?"

Weak at the knees, I said, "Well, with pâté de foie gras, of course. Success is in the timing of ingredients, and my timing is perfect." I winked at my soon-to-be wife, who had entered the room.

Steven grasped the innuendo and scowled at me. "Where do you get your pâté de foie gras?" He was practically out of his seat, boring into me with those grey-green hawk eyes.

"The pâté de foie gras?" I stuttered.

"Yes," he nodded. "Where do you get it?"

"Citerella."

"Citerella?"

He clearly didn't know the best specialty store in Manhattan. I felt redeemed.

"Yes, up on one hundred Twenty-Fifth Street?" I gloated. The place had been there over a century.

"Oh, I go all the way to Paris for mine." He sat back with a smile. "Cooking is not to be taken lightly."

What should have been common ground was now turning into a pissing match between us.

"How do you get to Paris?" I asked, knowing full well he couldn't leave the country. I looked to Adina for help. She sat quietly gazing out of the window.

He laughed. "Friends go a long way."

"Oh," I said, assuming, of course, he had intimidated half of Paris into sending him pâté de foie gras. Who had friends anymore?

"What about the Madeira?"

"What about it?" I said, agitated. I don't like to talk about my cooking; I just like to do it.

"Well, which do you use?"

"Sercial, corner wine store has a good one."

"Um, ever try Verdelho? Adds a better flavor. I get mine from Spain."

"You don't say?" I said, though I knew any good cook would use a Sercial Madeira for Wellington.

"Harry's Beef Wellington is delicious, Daddy." Adina came to my rescue, finally.

Cordova appeared to have taken a blow to the chest.

"I say we have a Beef Wellington tasting day then. What say you, Harry? Let's see whose specialty is better?"

I looked to Adina. "Do I have a chance?" I smiled

weakly.

Cordova sat there grinning at me. "Well?"

"Sure," I said. "But who will judge?"

"Why, my wife and my daughter."

I jumped from my seat. "That's unfair," I hollered. "They're unlikely to insult you."

Cordova sat back and laughed so heartily tears came to his eyes. "Oh, Harry, don't get so hot under the collar. I'm sure you make a fine Beef Wellington, not to my standards but fine enough."

"I'll invite my parents," I said indignantly. "Fair is fair."

"From what I hear, your father will be an excellent judge."

I sat fuming. I was about to marry his daughter and I detested him. What was he insinuating, that my fat father must be a food connoisseur?

Just at that moment, Julia Cordova swept through the room like a prima ballerina.

"I don't eat beef," she said as she twirled, a small dark woman who clearly liked to dance.

"Well, then how can you judge us?" I asked in amazement and looked at Adina, still grinning, surely taking pleasure from my pain.

Cordova got up and led his wife to a chair before she spun herself out of the window.

"She still knows a good tenderloin fillet when she tastes it." He winked at me and sat back down.

"Beef tenderloin? How do you get your hands on beef tenderloin?" I couldn't believe this. Most people had to wait years before getting an order of tenderloin, it was not only hard to get, but it was also incredibly expensive.

"How the hell else can you make Beef Wellington?" he asked.

"Chuck," I whimpered, knowing I'd been cut off at the knees. "Or sirloin."

"Jesus." He slumped in his chair. "Chuck or sirloin? And you're marrying my daughter?"

I shook my head in disbelief. He was preposterously rude. "You must have connections," I said.

"Of course, I have connections. How do you think I've lived this long?"

"I hadn't thought of that." I glared at him.

"I hope you're not planning to live in Adina's apartment. She has a lousy kitchen?"

"Well," I turned to Adina. "We might not be allowed to sell, isn't that right, sweetheart?"

"My kitchen is perfectly fine," Adina said.

"Ah." Cordova sighed deeply. "And what do you think of that, Harry?"

"It sucks, sir."

Julia Cordova got up, twirled twice around the room, and landed at the arm of my chair. Suddenly I found my head in her bosom.

"Poor dear," she said. "We all live under a cloud."

CHAPTER NINE

Adina

Edward gave a piano recital today, his first. My mother came to hear him play and Daddy caught the last stanza, which was Beethoven's 5th in C minor. The parents of some of the other children were in attendance, as well as a few siblings and servants. Edward's own parents, however, could not afford the time away from work. His mother is an ER nurse and rarely gets home before 2:00 A.M. His father produces the evening news, if you can call it that, and works even longer hours. I know his father well. We have teamed together many times to write, report and produce legitimate news, which we run through the underground station, accessible only through *Âme*'s subversive webcam. The commercial news Edward's father is forced to produce focuses on violence, punishment, financial gains, weather and sports. A good deal of world and local news is fiction, lies and propaganda.

001.0011.11.0011.01.011.011.1.0001.001.1.011.1.1.011.011.1.001.0001.11.1.001.001.001.1.1.011.11.001.1.001.001.000001.01.001.001.1.011.01.1.011.1.0001.011.001.00

Edward's face is full of pride. I can see how he looks for

his father in the small audience of invited guests, even though he knows neither of his parents is expected.

"I'm going to tell your father how good you were," I whispered and hugged him to me.

Physical contact is especially important, and when Edward threw his arms around my waist, I was overjoyed. In the past, he has always shied away from affection. Well, it would be a good day in more ways than one. Sara approached us tentatively, her head bowed, but still, I saw the blush on her face.

"You were good," she said and blushed more deeply.

Edward's smile widened. "Do you play?" he asked, as if noticing her for the first time.

Sara shook her head, and her eyes went to the floor. This was the only time I have heard Sara speak directly to another child.

"I can teach you," he offered.

She picked her head up sharply. Her eyes were round and blue as lapis lazuli. I watched as he studied her face, dimples deep as puddles, her blonde curls fell in ringlets on her brow. I knew how disappointed he'd be if she said 'no.' This little girl was quite a beauty.

"Yes," she whispered softly.

A deafening pounding broke the moment.

"Ouch," Edward squealed. The children and I ran to the piano. All other heads turned toward us. Bertram was banging on the keys, even trying to rip some out. I grabbed his hands.

"Stop that, Bertram."

I noticed his tight expression. His curled-back lips wrinkled his nose, making him comical, though I'm sure that wasn't his intention.

"Why should I stop? Edward plays it."

I sat down beside him on the bench. Sara and Edward stood next to me, still horrified at Bertram's behavior. "It's all right," I said to them. "Edward, before you teach Sara to play, why don't you show her your sheet music."

I handed him some sheet music and told him to take Sara to the couch. Bertram glared at me.

"Edward played music," I said. "You, on the other hand, produced noise." I wanted to brush the hair off his forehead, but I couldn't. He might have hit me.

"What's the difference?" he asked angrily.

"Listen." I played a few chords of something I knew. "Can you recognize it as music?"

"I guess."

Then I pounded the keys. "What I am doing?"

"Playing music," he said.

Acknowledging the challenge, I decided then and there that I would give a class on twentieth-century popular tunes, hoping Bertram would find an affinity, at least by the time we got to disco music.

I looked over at Sara and Edward and smiled. They were giggling over something or other. Then they started to sing. I was so happy to see such playfulness between them. I wondered what my eyes would have revealed if a little boy named Harry had wanted to teach me music years ago. I'm sure I would have blushed and giggled, as well.

01.001.11.001.101.111.01.1.0001.001.101.111.01.1.001.0001.11.1.001.001.001.11.01.11.001.1.001.0000001.01.001.001.101.11.11.01.1.00001.01.1.001.00

I have been married to Harry for two months now. Our wedding was beautiful, and since real honeymoons are prohibited, we stole an afternoon and went walking where the river used to run beside the park. Harry was such a handsome groom. I insisted he wore an old tuxedo, though no one gets married in them anymore. It makes me sad to watch so many weddings on television with brides in skirts so short, their bikini wax shows, and grooms revealing imperfect legs in shorts that hit their knees, or those awful nudist weddings that are so popular in Arizona. That would never work for Harry and me.

For our wedding, I wore my mother's wedding dress, white and long. Harry said it revealed my "high peaks" splendidly and he couldn't wait till the guests left.

My father insisted on catering our wedding: the food was so succulent that we salivated during our vows. We had a real cake that Daddy personally designed. It was five feet seven inches tall, with bells up the side and lovebirds at the top. Harry went to lick one of the wings and clipped it. I thought Daddy was going to kill him, but he controlled the impulse. I was so proud of him.

So, I am now Mrs. Harry Erin Cooper, and I could not be happier or feel more loved. Even Daddy admits, though always out of Harry's hearing, that I married a dear, dear prince of a man.

01.001.11.001.1.011.1.011.0001.001.1.011.1.1.011.001.0001.111.1.001.001.001.1.1.011.1.1.001.1.001.0000001.01.001.001.1.011.1.1.011.10001.01.1.001.00

My husband has taken two days off to prepare his Beef Wellington. I hope Daddy will not be too hard on him. We waited till after the wedding for the Beef Wellington Face-Off because Harry was working something out for tenderloin. It will probably cost him a year's rent.

During the recital, even from the secret room, my father's cooking was the most tantalizing aroma in the world. My father was, and is, an incredible chef, and at least, I have had that in my life. In a world that stinks of body odor and rot because of the limits on water, my father turns hell to heaven with a whisk, a pot and a spoon. But I must admit, my husband is no slouch either.

Daddy is likely to tease Harry unmercifully tonight after the Wellington contest, though I begged him not to. My father cannot pass up an opportunity to be outrageous. And much to my chagrin, as if not to prove me wrong, he entered the secret room with a magnum of Champagne and had the servants pass around the glasses.

"In honor of Maestro Edward," he said and poured Champagne into each glass.

Horrified, I sat there staring in disbelief. Finally, I screamed out, "Daddy, the children cannot drink Champagne!"

He gave me a huge grin and raised his glass. "To Edward," he said loudly.

Helplessly, I watched as each child toasted and gulped the Champagne as if it were a malted.

My father stopped sipping and walked to me with a skip, his usual gait.

"Well, they certainly could drink Champagne if they wanted to," he said. "but today they drink sparkling ginger ale from the Netherlands. Excellent brew," he whispered in my ear.

I breathed a sigh of relief and realized that no one in the room would have recognized Champagne, even if they really did have a glass of it. Champagne is far too expensive and can only be purchased through request. Most people don't bother because of the expense and the time it would take to get approval. Of course, Daddy got Champagne whenever he wanted it. Contacts, he always said, were the modern black market, friends of necessity.

As people began to leave, they stopped to say good-bye, asked me about Daddy's delightful smells from the kitchen, and thanked me for the Champagne. Even Bertram crinkled his nose again, but this time, he smiled.

"What's that?" he asked, sniffing like a long-snouted dog.

"Stew," Susan interjected.

I laughed out loud. If Daddy ever heard his Wellington referred to as stew, he'd have poor Susan and Bertram in the kitchen, deliciously amused with an education on the culinary arts. Perhaps not such a bad idea. I wondered how Harry was doing with his Wellington back at our apartment.

"Would you like to learn to cook?" I asked Bertram.

He looked at me as if I were crazy.

82

"Ask him," he said, pointing at Edward. "I don't cook."

"There's nothing wrong with cooking," I added, to which Bertram made a face.

The results of most of his tests indicate that if he matures in our present society, he'll most likely become an engineer. But if he finds something he likes better, he could shift; there was still time, as long as Bertram had the aptitude for whatever he chose.

Defining just what Bertram's aptitudes were was a work in progress. I thought it was important for the children to choose their destiny themselves. The twins, Michelle and Omiyinka, were both math wizards and, most likely, faced futures in the financial markets. Sam could paint, but fine art was no longer valued; we would have to move him to France, if he wanted to pursue his talent. Sara and Bertram were still undecided. One thing I knew for sure about Bertram, though: his aptitude would not be for music.

CHAPTER TEN

We found out, only days before our wedding, that The Brain had refused our request to sell Adina's apartment. So, we made the best of it by redecorating. We compromised and knocked out part of the dining room wall to expand the space, leaving us with a small, but still formal, room, and I'd have a place for my pots and knives in our extended kitchen.

Steven and I continued to spar with one another. I think he enjoyed baiting me, controlling and unnerving me. Fortunately, my parents found him charming, at least.

I was nervous the night of the Beef Wellington Cook-Off, which Cordova, of course, insisted upon. At my request, my parents were invited to participate in the challenge. I wasn't about to do this without a fan base of my own.

01.001.11001.1.01.1.11.01.1.0001.001.1.01.1.1.01.1.001.0001.1.1.1.001.001.001.1.1.01.1.1001.1.001.000001.01.001.001.1.01.1.1.01.1.10001.01.1.001.00

When Adina and I arrived for the awaited evening, my father was already settled on the couch and my mother was playing the piano for Julia, who twirled around the room to some old music that must have been popular in my mother's youth, 'Yo, Man, But Yo Mama Beasting Out On Me' – just perfect for the rats.

My poor father held his ears as inconspicuously as

possible.

"Hi, Dad," I said as I kissed him on the cheek. With a surreptitious wink, I glanced in Julia's direction and pointed my chin. "She likes to dance," I whispered.

"I see that." Father winced. "But now that we're all among friends, how about something more humane, like Chopin?"

Cordova, sitting across the room from Father, laughed. He wore an apron with *Bard of Beef Wellington* written across it. He grinned mischievously at his wife, who twirled into his arms with a breathless thud.

"My little ballerina," Cordova said as he slapped her derrière, "likes to rock and roll."

I heard my mother's call above the music as my wife walked toward me.

"Darling," Mother sang out.

I instinctively opened my arms to my mother, for I hadn't seen her in a week, but she was not referring to me.

Adina and Mother met midway in the center of the room and clutched each other like rescued hikers after an avalanche. We hadn't seen the Cordovas since our wedding, but it might have been years the way they hugged and kissed.

"My sweet daughter-in-law," Mother exclaimed. "Loved her from the moment I saw her," she told Cordova. "I said to my Harry that he had found the girl of his dreams and I insisted he ping her. Oh, she has such beautiful eyes."

"Good choice," Cordova said.

I stood there with the Wellington in a Tupperware, not knowing what to say. Mother never ceased to amaze me. If I remember correctly, she thought Adina's eyes had been shifty.

"I'm going to take my Wellington into the kitchen," I said sheepishly.

"You do that, Harry." Cordova sniffed the air. "There's

no aroma," he said. "What you got there, Harry? Dog rations?"

I clenched my teeth. "You're going to be pleasantly surprised, Steven," I said, trying to maintain my sense of humor. "I'm going to beat the pants off you."

His loud and overbearing guffaws followed me out of the room.

Well, Adina and I were laughing like fools as well. I had been able to purchase beef tenderloin from my greedy boss, who had taken my two-week summer vacation for payment, but I was sure it would be worth it. I was sure to be the star of the evening.

The entire apartment carried the aromas of heaven, if there is one – cooking onions, sauce, and meat. Since both our pots were in the oven, I couldn't tell which one was faring better, Steven's or mine. But the succulence of it all was immense and I could barely think.

Not only was Steven privy to beef tenderloin, but he was also able to get his hands on Baron de Rothschild Lègende Bordeaux Rouge, at, I was told, only five hundred dollars a bottle.

"You like?" Steven asked as he filled my glass.

"Love is more like it." I grinned.

"Ah, you have a fine taste for wine, son," Steven said. "It seems we have a lot in common," he added.

"It seems we do." I smiled at Adina.

Steven caught our exchange and laughed. "Oh, yes, of course, we both love Adina. But I meant food and wine, Harry. I would never allow Adina to marry a vegan, heaven forbid."

My father laughed. Cole Porter was piping in from somewhere, but I couldn't tell exactly where the speakers were. The music had the effect of a drug on my father, who grinned foolishly as he sang along. I, on the other hand, didn't quite get, "you're Mahatma Gandhi, you're the nose on the great Durante." Who the hell are those people?

"Do you like the music, Rory?" Steven asked my father, who nodded dreamily.

"Do you have Cole Porter's collection?" Father asked.

"His and Berlin's," Steven said.

"Ah, how very nice." Father smiled in Mother's direction, who nodded approvingly.

Steven's taste was incredibly olde worlde, cut crystal wine glasses and rugs with Persian designs. Tapestries hung from the wall and looked authentic, worth thousands; I was sure.

The art was Impressionist. The Brain had denounced the Impressionists, many of them relegated to the soul file for having too much mood and emotion. I was eager to study Steven's Manet, confident it was an original. Our own modern art was grotesque and obvious, so much sexual innuendo in geometric dissected penises and breasts in abstract, very Picasso, an artist the brain still allowed.

The evening was pleasant. Mrs. Cordova danced, of course. At one point, Mother got up and joined her and we watched as the two twirled together to Irving Berlin's "Cheek to Cheek." At least I found that song easier to understand.

"So what did you make of the androids?" I heard Cordova ask me.

My father looked at us with an amused tilt to his head. "Androids?" he asked. "Too many of them, they get in my way."

"Well, three of them accompanied my daughter to dinner." Cordova got up and filled my father's glass.

My father laughed. "They don't eat," he said.

"Well, apparently, some do." Cordova looked at his daughter. "Have they ever contacted you again?"

Adina shook her head. "They told me there will be a financial collapse," she said to my father.

My father looked surprised. "Really? Well, I suppose it's possible."

"How so?" Cordova asked. "The Brain would never permit it."

"Perhaps The Brain is an android," I said. "Or a holograph." I heard Adina laugh.

"Holographs reflect someone. So, even if The Brain is a holograph, and we could see it, it would be someone," Adina said.

Cordova shook his head. "Someone? Or nothing?" he asked.

I looked at him as though he were crazy, but when I thought about it, perhaps it wasn't so farfetched.

"They ought to outlaw those damn things," my father said. "The androids are bad enough … but those holographs? Downright macabre."

01.0011.11.001.1.011.11.01.1.0001.001.1.011.11.01.1.001.1.0001.11.1.001.001.001.1.1.011.1.001.1.001.0000001.01.001.001.1.01.1.1.1.01.1.00001.01.1.001.00

At long last, the moment arrived for me to prove that I was the better chef. I would not berate Steven, or make him feel bad, but I would, of course, offer to teach him how to improve. I knew he had been a professional chef all his life, but he'd been retired for years. Surely, he was rusty. The Brain taught us that youth surpasses age, simply because youth progresses and leaves behind what is no longer useful or modern. Modern is always better, according to The Brain.

Why, I'll bet that Steven isn't even aware the Wellington crust can be purchased at Wal-Mart.

The robot servants had set the table beautifully with candelabras at both ends and the light muted and subtle. The Cordovas had even placed nametags on the pretty set china plates.

"Now then," Cordova said. "You two lovely people will sit here." He pointed to my mother and father.

They sat in the chairs that faced the view of what was once the Hudson River. I watched as Steven tied black satin nightshades around their heads, covering their eyes.

"Oh, that's nifty," I said, giving Adina a wink.

Steven seated his daughter and me on the other side of the table. He and Julia took the end places. I was instructed to cover my eyes with the satin nightshades, which I did.

"Harry's Wellington will be served on plates bordered by grey flowers and my Wellington will be served on plates bordered by pink flowers. We'll count the flowers at the end of the tasting and see whose Wellington takes the prize."

The redolent excitement at the prospect of beef tenderloin was overwhelming, and I wet my lips, relishing the opportunity to beat Steven at his own game.

I heard Steven instruct the servants to bring out the Wellingtons. I detected excitement in his voice.

"I am putting on my night shades now. This is how it will work. My good Leeza will feed us the first Wellington. I have no idea which one it will be, yours or mine, Harry. But your Wellington is on the plate bordered in grey and my Wellington on the plate bordered in pink, as I mentioned."

We heard the servants wheel in the dishes and place them on the table.

"First, Leeza, serve my wife, if you will."

We waited and listened, as Mrs. Cordova tasted the first Wellington.

"Oh, my," she said. "I like this one."

"You haven't tasted the second one yet, dear." Steven said.

"I don't need to," she said. "I like this one."

"All right, dear. Leeza, take the other dish away and leave the first one."

"Yes, sir."

"I don't believe that's fair," I said.

"You're next, Harry." Steven cleared his throat and ignored my comment. I hope your gustatory talents are in full swing."

"I can't wait," I said and lifted the fork to my mouth. The meat melted like butter and I swooned, deliriously satisfied, salivating for more. The crust was so soft I might have licked my plate, intoxicated with the flavor, the subtle hint of Madeira.

"This is quite good," I said.

"Second dish, if you will, Leeza," Steven instructed. "Please cleanse your palette with water."

I swallowed some water and Leeza placed the fork in my hand; I brought the meat to my mouth: my nose suggested it was slightly burnt. Next, I tasted the crust: slightly dry. The sauce lacked the subtle flavor of the Madeira. I laughed nervously. "This is exceedingly difficult." I blushed as I said it. "Let me reflect on this."

"We are blindfolded and hungry, Harry. Please state the dish you would like Leeza to remove," Steven insisted.

"Yes, sir," I said, "the first one."

The tasting continued around the table until we had each had had a turn.

"All right now," Steven said. "Off with your shades."

I stared around me. The remaining dishes were bordered in pink flowers, all except mine, bordered in grey.

Steven smiled at me and shook his head slowly. "You can't be serious, Harry."

"No, sir," I laughed. I looked for Leeza and caught her eyes. "If you will, please bring me a plate of Mr. Cordova's Beef Wellington."

Adina looked at me pathetically. Mother sighed. Father wore a contrived expression, but he winked at me, as if to say "now don't take this too seriously, son."

"Harry, Harry, Harry," Steven said. "You have potential. I'll teach you how to be as good as me, don't worry."

After dinner, we retreated into the living room. I had finished enough wine to soothe my hurt feelings and I smiled at Steven as he handed me a glass of port.

"Who's handling your money?" he asked.

"Kripling," I said.

"Kripling wouldn't survive a blow. Not a good choice."

"What are you talking about?" I asked and looked at Adina. "Is there a blow coming our way? Did those robot cretins really know something?"

"Does it really matter who handles our money, Father?" Adina sipped on her Crème de Cacao and didn't answer me. "We are relegated to allowances anyway. If one person goes broke, we probably all will."

"Ah, yes, my good daughter. We all have allowances," Steven said. "And the illusion of individual wealth."

Then my father piped in. "Let me ask you this, if The Brain were to go broke what would happen?"

We all looked at him. That still seemed a bit absurd.

"We'd be relegated to the institutions," Adina said and shuddered.

"We'd annihilate The Brain, wouldn't we? What if we took all the money out of our accounts?" Steven asked. "How many of us could be imprisoned at one time?"

"No, that's not the way to stop The Brain," Father said. "The money we have is an illusion anyway."

"What do you mean?" Adina asked. "Because it isn't ours, it doesn't exist?"

"Well," my father began. "We think we're rich, but we aren't. Who owns the banks?"

"Are you saying The Brain has all the money?" Adina asked. "Then why are some people poor and not us?"

"I'm saying we believe we have something which is only predicated on having nothing." My father poured himself another glass of port and helped himself to a handful of chocolate mints. "The Brain inherited our fortunes. It owes us everything, but we never see the benefits. The more time we give to it, the more money we get for it. But if we were to stop working for The Brain, we'd be paupers inside of five seconds."

"If we moved The Brain's money somewhere else, what would happen?" Steven asked.

"The Brain would dissolve unless it's been backed up to such a degree that it would only upload its losses, and eventually retaliate. That's my job, to protect those assets." My father chewed on the chocolate and licked it from his fingers. "To stop The Brain, you'd have to move the money away and drown the source, or sell everything for cash before The Brain got wind of it. You can't give it anything to back up."

"Can it be done?" Steven asked. "I mean, the money must go somewhere."

"Well, it's possible," my father said. "To hide it."

"Just what exactly do you do, Rory?" Steven stood up and went to his computer. He appeared to be changing the music.

"I'm a technician," my father said.

"You don't say?"

"Well, yes, I build computers, replicas of The Brain's agenda."

Steven picked up the port and walked to the library doors. "You and I should have a chat, Rory. Let our children enjoy the evening, the music and the moonlight."

I watched as Steven led my father into the library and closed the doors behind them. Adina's look was indecipherable, but her eyes remained on the space her father had left. I watched her until she was conscious of my gaze. Julia danced to another Cole Porter song. Adina smiled. I smiled back at my wife as Julia twirled and dipped and glided before us.

CHAPTER ELEVEN

Adina

Sam's paintings are on the wall. Some remind me of deserts, dry but mystical. One is of lone flowers in a field of dust and another of prairie wolves that look out of hungry, yellow eyes and snarl. My favorite is the one of stars, glittering in sand as if the sky opened and let them fall. There are castles the color of shells, their moats misplaced and empty, pyramids that tumble and bend on city streets. He paints what he feels, and he sees what others don't.

Sometimes, wonders never cease. Sara has kissed Edward on the collar of his shirt and on his arm, the chocolate she consumed at lunch, a smudge in the crease, a silhouetted kiss. A brown smear that makes him grin. He plays the piano, and she follows badly, but to Edward he has heard a chord from Mozart's hands.

There are wonders that play upon the mirrors in the secret room and reflect smiles and laughter. Children's stories enacted by Michelle, who twirls like my mother and speaks to a prince who isn't there. Kittens that curl in

Omiyinka's lap and purr. I can see the sweetness in her eyes as she strokes the fur; adorable and cute, the kitten licks her hand.

"Scratchy," she says. "Like salt crystals."

These children are the antithesis of The Brain. I take some credit for this. It is I who has helped lead them to this place – imagination and music, literature, and art – all the beauty The Brain has erased with its dark, pernicious pencil. Watching these children is like finding a pearl in black dirt, discovering air in the consumption of a fire. In my mind, I see a tornado of smoke, and inside, the Computer Project melts, and The Brain disintegrates into a substance of insignificant value.

Wonders make me smile. No, Bertram has no fine ear for piano playing but the child can sing. My God, he can sing. He wants to be a rocker, he told me, as he thrashed about threatening to kill and smash whatever stood in his way – popular lyrics of a new song. The violent meaningless lyrics of a generation reared on too many years of deafening anger. But we have an underground of music, Bertram. If you can imagine drifting in space, it would be called the melody of time. And the voices that linger beyond the harp and the violin are sweet. Love this music, Bertram, this lost music. I must teach this gifted singer to sing, not wail, not threaten, nor rape and abuse, but sing.

Wonders, wonders and more wonders that never cease, I am pregnant. I am not only pregnant, but I am also deliriously happy. In the beginning, I was afraid. Educate my child by Computer Project? How can I? But joy and elation are so much stronger than fear. Harry was saved. I was saved. We will protect our children, as well. I anticipate the birth of my child to such a degree that I can think of nothing else. I try to imagine my baby's face, to envision the expression the first time it cries, to hold it when it hurts and see its eyes embrace me when I soothe it. I am pregnant,

94

soon to populate a barren world with a gift it will never receive, not if I have anything to do with it. This child is ours, Harry's and mine. The Brain's eerie fingers will never stroke it.

"Children," I call to my students and they gather around me with faces that anticipate only the positive, the absurd and ridiculous, because I have taught them to laugh.

"I'm pregnant," I say, not that it's a laughing matter, or perhaps it is.

Bertram's eyes widen. "Yuck."

"Wow," say Omiyinka and Michelle almost at once.

"Congratulations, Mrs. Cooper," Edward says politely, and with a blush to his white cheeks.

"Can I hold it when it's born?" asks Sara.

"Of course," I say and sit her on my lap.

I look for my little artist. He stands alone, crying, my sensitive little Sam.

"Sam?" I said. "I'm going to have a baby."

And my sweet little artist puts his arms around me and cries even louder.

"If I could paint the soul, and God, and all the angels," he finally manages to get out, "it would look like your baby. It would glow as pure."

"And if I could paint wondrous, handsome, mysterious love," I whispered, "it would look like you."

"This is the way it should be?" he asks me. "Shouldn't it?"

CHAPTER TWELVE

"So my daughter is about to give me a grandchild," Steven said the evening we brought the good news of our first child.

Adina and I had been married a year by this time. The Brain allowed us two children, but we didn't want any, not at first. We used birth control religiously, if you'll pardon my terminology ... an expression I picked up from the soul file. We refused to subject our children to a Computer Project Education and that was all there was to it. We were afraid of what might happen to them under the influence of The Brain's poor excuse for knowledge. Not all children were affected, of course, but how could we know that ours wouldn't be, especially if the cause was not only emotional but environmental?

The Brain could not force us to have children, though our taxes would rise if we reached forty and remained childless. But we would not put our children at risk for emotional and mental damage, even if it meant financial cuts. Becoming parents was out of the question for us, that is, before it happened.

One careless night, after a gluttonous dinner, my eyes locked with Adina's. It was around dessert: strawberry shortcake with chocolate truffles and fresh cream. Suddenly, we found ourselves on the floor, feeding each other with our hands, licking the cream from each other's face, sucking on the truffles and passing them back and forth in our mouths. I undressed her slowly, taking in her gorgeous body, now covered in my homemade cream. We fell into an idyllic trance. She slipped off my pants and spread strawberries into my inner thigh. I slowly rubbed the shortcake on her naked stomach until her chocolate hands found my peppered penis. We fell into intercourse like pumped-up teenagers in the backseat of an abandoned Buick.

Adina announced she was pregnant shortly thereafter, and all our misgivings went out the window. It was splendid news, despite our fears. We danced on air, like Julia Cordova; we spun as we thought of it. We were going to be parents, and we'd worry about the consequences later.

0100011100110111011110010000100100111101100100011110011001001101110111001100100000001010010011011110110100011011001100

I noticed that Steven was more morose than usual. I thought news of his first grandchild would temper him and quiet his appetite for torturing me. How wrong I was.

"And if it's a boy?"

We were alone in the large sitting room. Adina and her mother had gone off to the kitchen to put on some coffee; made to the specifications of Mr. Cordova's demands, I might add, always with a little shaved chocolate and hazelnuts.

"Sir?"

"What will you name it?"

"Oh, well, we've decided on Timothy."

"Timothy?"

"Yes, sir."

"Who the hell is that?"

"No one, we just like the name."

"I don't."

That stunned me. Now the son of a bitch wanted to name

my first-born child?

"No offense, sir, but I'm not fond of the name Steven. Adina and I discussed it and we prefer to remain neutral. I'm not even naming our son after my father, though I like the name Rory."

"Well, good for you but not my question."

"Sir?"

"And if it's a girl?"

"We like Beth."

"Pshaw."

"Excuse me?"

"Beth rhymes with death."

"What?" I could not believe the audacity of this fool who, unfortunately, was my dear wife's father.

"Timmy rhymes with gimme. Is that what you want in a son? Gimme, gimme, gimme? Gimme Timmy?"

"Are you all right, sir? I can get you an aspirin." I said, getting up. He must be losing his mind.

"Theodore Roosevelt was a fine president, a real man's man. Teddy is solid, like being ready. Ready Teddy."

I looked at him in disbelief, as he had the nerve to continue.

"Lindsey was my mother's name, an exceptionally fine woman. She had the grace of a swan. Lindsey like flimsy, fluid."

I finally got it. "You want me to name my son Theodore and if it's a girl, Lindsey, is that it?"

He put his hand on my shoulder. "Won't be the only thing I'm going to ask of you, son."

I clenched my teeth. I loved my wife, but her parents were out there. Still, she was as determined to please them as I was to please mine, so I understood.

"I'll discuss it with Adina," I said.

"Good enough," he said and kissed my cheek.

Steven Cordova got his request and we named our son after Theodore Roosevelt and when Adina became pregnant again, after a night of tenderloin, sherbet and chocolate mousse, our daughter was named after Steven Cordova's mother. Steven wasn't lying about making more requests of me, either.

"Under no circumstances will you raise my grandchildren with Computer Project educations," he bellowed.

I certainly agreed with him, but I saw no way around it. This was the world we lived in. This was the future our children had to adopt. I told Steven that we would not destroy their soul files. We would protect them as we had been protected. But I don't think that answer was good enough for Steven Cordova.

01.001.1.1.001.1.01.1.1.01.1.0001.001.1.01.1.1.1.01.1.001.0001.1.1.1.001.001.001.1.1.01.1.1.001.1.001.0000001.01.001.001.1.01.1.1.01.1.00001.01.1.001.00

Adina had been happy while carrying Teddy. But things changed by the time she was pregnant with Lindsey. We realized that Teddy would be ready for preschool by the time Lindsey was born, and it weighed on both our minds. We'd have to enroll him in the Computer Project or risk going to court and losing our child. If we refused, we'd be stripped of our income altogether. We'd be desolate and if our parents took us in, they'd be cut to the bone, as well.

As the months passed, Adina's mood shifted as quietly as clouds running aimlessly across a sky, leaving rain in their wake. I didn't know exactly what she was thinking, but wished I could decipher the gravity of them. They were impressions that found buoyancy in dark waters, and weight in the quiet corners of her mind. I didn't pressure her to share her thoughts, which was a good thing. But, eventually, of course, she did.

"What are you thinking, Adina?" I asked.

"You know what I'm thinking, Harry. I won't subject our children to harm."

Adina looked out of the window. It was dusk and the sun was a burst of waning exuberance. I watched, as the fading light caught her eyes and revealed an unsettling determination: the eyes of a female tiger around her threatened cubs.

"We discussed this, Adina. What choice do we have? There must be a way to counter what our children are taught. My parents did it for me. Your parents did it for you. I don't see any other way for them."

She shook her head. "That's not entirely what concerns me.

"What if we request permission to raise our children abroad?" I asked as I took her hand. There was so much less Computer Project influence in Europe and many more underground schools. I hoped that would please her, remove the shadows of fear that I felt. We'd risk it. We'd go to Europe.

"Our request will be denied, Harry." She sighed and looked at me in defeat. "And if we rebel against that decision and go anyway, we'll be broke. They'll cut us off from everything we own."

"Look, you'll educate them just as you educate your students." I slammed my fist on the countertop. "What hellish world are we living in?"

"How can we protect them from the violence, Harry?"

"I don't know."

"Children are becoming more and more disassociated. It gets worse year after year. How can we protect our children from these horrible influences?"

Now that I was a fully fledged member of *Âme,* I was privy to actual news, so I knew what was really going on in the world. Daily I accessed a news site and read how children were killing randomly. The only attachments they formed were to technology, inanimate objects and their own hungers. If they wanted something, they only had to point a pistol at whatever stood in the way, and it was theirs. Pistols were readably available. We all had to own them to protect ourselves from the homeless, who often tried to rob us.

"What the hell are we going to do?" I asked.

Adina looked at me with the same expression I'd seen on people stripped of their livelihood by The Brain: profound fear.

"We have to sneak out of the country, Harry. We have to find a way to do it, somehow."

She seemed out of control, driven to believe in any reckless decision that would grant us a normal life.

"But we'll never get back in," I said. "Our children will never know their grandparents. We'll be destitute, unable to find work in France, or anywhere else in Europe. You know The Brain will blacklist us. Is it worth it? *Âme* is not going to support us, Adina."

She came to me and put her arms around my neck. She buried her head in my shoulder for a long time. I stroked the silken hair that touched my lips, breathed in the only hints of what was clean and crisp. For outside our windows, the city stank of rot.

She raised her eyes to mine. "I think Daddy has a plan … I just don't know what it is."

"What do you mean?"

"I'm not sure. He hasn't been himself lately, but he's acting like a man with a diabolical mental malfunction."

"What could Steven possibly spring on us?"

I knew that was a loaded question. My father-in-law could convince the profoundly stable into acts of unimaginable insanity.

"I think he might want us to leave the city."

"What, and live with the poor?" I smiled at her. One thing I could not believe was that Steven would want us to subject ourselves to bad food, people who rarely got permission to bathe and apartments smaller than an engagement-ring box. On the other hand, could our children really escape the dark knoll of a bleak bell that permeated the city streets? There weren't any guarantees... or answers.

01001110011101111011000100110111101110010001110010011100110010000000101001001101111011100010111001100

Steven Cordova was full of surprises. It wasn't long after the birth of our daughter that he sat me down over lunch at the Twenty-One Club.

"It's time to re-evaluate your life, son," he said.

"Look, sir, I prefer not to have this argument again. Adina and I have decided not to risk it, sneaking out of the country will cost us our livelihood. I hope you understand. We'll have to watch the children closely, of course, but I'm sure we'll be able to keep them from harm, both mentally and emotionally."

"Not here, you won't."

"Besides, we'd never want to keep Teddy and Lindsey from their grandparents. By George, family is everything, sir, and if we go to Europe, we'll never return. You and Julia will never see the children again, unless you go with us, but I doubt if you'd make it as far as the airfield. You're blacklisted."

"Ha," he said. "They call it The Brain because it will always outsmart you, Harry."

I looked at him, trying to meet his eyes, though I knew my expression was thoroughly ridiculous. Just the effect he had on me.

"Harm is everywhere you look," he said. "I know you think that Julia and I are off our rockers, but we do know things … makes us squirrely, I suppose."

I wondered what in the world he thought he knew that no one else did, aside from the art of making one hell of a Beef Wellington.

"You were a Computer Project baby," he said.

I wondered where he was going with this. Every child of the upper class was a recipient of the Computer Project. "Of course," I said. "What else could my parents have done?"

"Julia and I left the country to protect Adina. You could still leave America thirty years ago. Now, it's impossible. But The Brain is a cancer, Harry. You can't subject your children to it. I know, I know, you went through the Computer Project and survived, but The Brain is far more powerful now than it was when it first began. You barely survived, Harry."

"Adina approves of my upbringing," I said. "I have all my files. My parents saw to it. We can do the same for our children."

His remarks agitated me and he must have felt it. He reached for my hand.

"Yes, yes, you had wonderful parents, Harry, but they're not the point of this conversation. You do realize, don't you, that at any time we can find ourselves with a bullet in our brain. Do you understand me, Harry?"

He exhausted me. I knew the danger, but what the hell could I do about it. Lampoon every ten-year-old on rollerblades?

"Of course, Steven."

He leaned in close to me. "I'm dying, young man," he said. "Let's get to the subject of interest. I don't know how long I have, days or hours."

I looked at him over the rim of my wine glass and wondered if he was trying to use his death to influence me to do something I didn't want to do. Hadn't he already named my children? Now what? Did he want to lay claim to my future, insist we leave the country and live like paupers?

"What could you possibly be dying from Steven, everything is curable?"

"Everything but two strains of cancer. I have one of them."

"Adina said it wasn't serious."

"When I'm ready to tell her, I'll tell her," he said.

As it slowly seeped in that he might be telling the truth, a profound sadness overcame me. "I'm really sorry," I said.

I meant that. Despite getting on my nerves, he'd grown on me. He wasn't a bad guy, just an annoying one.

"Do you love my daughter?" he asked.

"Yes," I answered. "Very much."

Steven took a sip of water. "I wonder if there's hope for you, Harry," he said.

"What the hell do you mean, 'hope for me?'"

"Three things," he said and held up three fingers. He then proceeded to lay out the rules of inheritance. They made no sense. He insisted on giving Adina and me a deed to some old house that he wanted me to promise to raise my family in. The house was in some godforsaken place called Pindar Corners, and then he mumbled something about a crisis.

"You'll have no other choice," he adamantly declared.

"I don't care about my wife's inheritance." I looked out over the room. What the hell was he getting at? "I'm already rich."

"Listen to me, Harry."

I took a deep breath. I did not like naming my children based on my father-in-law's choice instead of my own. Adina and I had fought for days over it. I didn't want to fight with my wife again. Adina was persuasive, but not enough that I would raise my family in some old house upstate, no matter who insisted on it.

"You will lose everything, Harry," he said.

I held back the tendency to laugh. We didn't lose in my world. Money was made, never lost.

"It will come crashing down on top of you, and not even Europe will be a safe haven. I can promise you that."

For the first time, he had a wild look in his eyes. I was afraid. The man was an expert on cooking, not economics. But still, something about his tone unnerved me.

"Your money in stocks, Harry?"

"The very best," I said. "Some blue-chip, some solar."

"Your job secure?"

"I'm a cartoonist. Comic relief. I create a better world, give people heroes, just like The Brain gives us caricatures of kings and presidents."

Steven reacted as though I had said something funny and chuckled.

"Why are you so amused?" I asked. "That's just the way it is."

"No, it's just the way you see it," he said, suddenly serious, depressingly so; his skin seemed sallow.

"What are you talking about, Steven?" I turned to look for the waiter. I wanted another glass of wine. I didn't know if my father-in-law had the urge to pretend he was psychic, or actually had some old man's disease, like senility.

"Pindar Corners is where you need to go," he said. "It will provide you with a safety net for a while. You think the city is safe? Then stay. Your children will wind up being eaten or blown away by other children … is that what you want?"

I stared at him in utter disbelief. "How can you say that? All I think about is protecting them from all harm."

"Pindar Corners, Harry."

"Pindar Corners? What the hell is that?"

Steven leaned over the table. I looked into his large hawk eyes, misty leaden hollows.

"Listen, there's going to be a virus," he said. "It's will blow the shit out of The Brain."

At this point, I wanted to abandon the 8 oz. sirloin that was coming my way. I wanted out. What the hell game was he playing? People like Steven are just too damn intense. I've never been comfortable around intensity.

"Look, Steven, I don't mean to be rude, but I don't know what you're getting at. I don't want to live in fucking Pindar Corners, wherever that is."

"Pindar Corners is in upstate New York."

"What? Adina and I can't live in upstate New York."

Upstate New York is where most of the institutions were for the poor. Rich people didn't go there, unless they were old. They had the old age farms up there, as well.

Steven reached out and grabbed my arm. His hand clutched me with surprising strength.

"I'm a psychic, Harry. I know your future. So do you. For God's sake, man. We created it."

In that second, I thought I might have to call for an ambulance: he was clearly insane.

"Tomorrow, it will all come crashing down around you. You want the cash? You want survival? You come to me, Harry or you'll drown along with everybody else. Make sure you get to me before I drop, though. This is for my grandchildren … and my daughter, and even for you. Don't waste too much time, damn it!"

I laughed uncomfortably, which is my way, I guess. I wanted to stand. He was clearly a crazy man; he was, without a doubt, *muy loco*, he was *fou*, *pazzo*, nuts.

CHAPTER THIRTEEN

But he wasn't. The very next day, the markets crashed, just as Steven said they would. It was unbelievable. Adina had the news on when I awoke. She sat in front of the computer like a zombie.

"How did he know this would happen?" I asked as I sat beside her and listened, watching the fear in the eyes of the broadcaster intensify.

"Check our statements, Harry." Adina was clearly nervous and rose to her feet.

I logged in quickly. It took only a second to access my account at Kriplings. "We're dead broke," I said as I surveyed all zero balances. I looked up in complete astonishment. Adina covered her face with her hands and looked about to fall to the floor.

"Our stocks are worthless, so are the bonds." I collapsed onto the couch. "How could this happen?" I asked. Sweat broke out all over my body. "It must be a malfunction, that's all."

"What did my father say to you?" She knelt before me and I knew what she was thinking

I relayed our conversation, as much of it as I could

remember.

"We've got to take the money, Harry. We've got to get out of Manhattan," she said. "Father told me what would happen. He told me to believe those androids and their stupid prophesy."

I looked at her helplessly, frozen in place.

"Harry? The roof has fallen in on us. Call your parents."

My mouth fell open, and still, the rest of my body would not move. This wasn't really happening, was it?

"Harry!" she screamed at me, startling me into action and I went to the phone.

"What did you have to do with this?" I asked and listened to my father's sigh.

Something about the night of the Beef Wellington Face-Off resurfaced in my memory, my father and Cordova going off behind the library doors. Yes, of course, my father was a computer genius; perhaps all he'd needed all along was a madman's plan.

My father remained silent but continued to sigh.

"We've lost everything," I said in disbelief. "Every golden penny I had in investments, every piece of property I owned," I shouted, my voice rising to boiling point levels.

"Unfortunately, there was a glitch," I heard him say.

"What are you talking about?"

He paused, obviously debating whether he should tell me anything. I was relieved to hear him speak.

"Only The Brain was supposed to fail, not the independent markets, not Wall Street. We figured out a way to deplete The Brain's resources and wipe them out altogether, but it backfired. We were only going to delete selected information, but as we worked on deleting files that came directly from The Brain's financial portfolio, some huge error report appeared, and my screen went blank a second later. The whole system crashed. I don't know what happened."

"What are you telling me?" I screamed.

"Everything got deleted. Look, Harry, I found the source of The Brain."

"What is it? Where is it?"

"It's running on its own power. Its source is omnipotent."

Unable to believe what he'd just said, I looked at my wife helplessly.

"We've lost the apartment. Our pensions and stock options are worthless. We meant to crush The Brain, only The Brain, not the whole frigging city."

I heard the tears in my father's voice. I felt a thousand things at once, but mostly rage; not at my father, but at this incipient monster that didn't even seem to derive from flesh and blood.

"We didn't stop to think that there's some power behind the fucking thing … somewhere. He or she or it … retaliated against us almost immediately."

"Look, we have to act fast. Don't leave the house," I hollered. "Wait for my call but pack your things. Just bring the basics."

"What, where are we going?"

"We're getting out of the city as quickly as possible, to a place called Pindar Corners."

After I hung up the phone, I found Adina standing by the window seemingly in a frozen state, as if covered in snow.

"If we don't get out soon, we might be killed," she said, staring out over Amsterdam Avenue. "I'm scared, Harry."

I put my arms around her. We looked back at the computer. All over the country, it was the same. The news was blaring and stark. The banks were closing right and left.

"The only available jobs will be menial, or so-called government positions, maybe teaching. There must be endless requests for those jobs already," I said.

From our walls, the computer newscast blared:

"The Upper class has vanished in a heartbeat and no one knows why or what has brought on this horrific attack."

I knelt before my wife. "Do you think our fathers …?"

She ran her hand through my hair. "They're already blaming a computer virus for the entire financial collapse," she said.

"What do you think will happen?" I asked.

"The Brain will re-emerge and promise assistance in the form of government checks and rebates. All our fathers succeeded in doing was killing the rich, not The Brain."

01001111001101111011000100011011111011001110011100110011001000000101001001101111011000010111001100

When America went broke in 2048, I was thirty-four years old. The only skill I had was as a cartoonist, and the publishing houses had all pulled the plug on our logins, as I discovered that morning. I had nowhere to go. The Computer Projects for Learning and Living were the only corporations still hiring technicians to man them. Though I'm very smart, I don't have the knack for technology. The bread lines were forming, and the disaster was only a few hours old.

"We've got the inheritance, Harry. We'll be safe," Adina said. "We've got to take my father up on his offer."

Needless to say, in lieu of a building to jump from …

"I agree," I told my wife softly.

01001111001101111011000100011011111011001110011100110011001000000101001001101111011000010111001100

"I'll do it," I said, finding Steven in bed, his face ashen, his large eyes suddenly small. "Pindar Corners, here we come."

"Can't take the heat, huh?"

"How did you know this was going to happen?"

"I told you, I'm psychic."

He handed me some papers to sign before giving me his will.

"Be a good boy, Harry, and sign."

"I don't know what to say," I said.

"Harry," he said. "I've just given you and Adina a small fortune. Use it wisely."

"Thank you." I leaned in close.

"Save your family. I trust you to do that. I always meant to leave the house to Adina, but I don't know what she'll do with it. You know how she is, very headstrong. That's why it's got to be in your name as well. Promise me, you'll never sell it."

"Yes, yes," I said. "I promise."

"You must help the children. No more Brain erasure. There is a way to beat it, Harry. Follow the yellow brick road. There'll be a man … he'll come to you in a dream. Don't reject him, Harry."

I looked at him helplessly. Maybe I had gone to the twilight zone.

"The Brain will always reboot," he said. "Unless you destroy it. Somewhere in Pindar Corners, it's there. The whole fucking thing. I don't know how I know that ... or perhaps, maybe I do. The closer you get to death, the more it all starts making sense. If you find it, Harry, pull the fucking wires one by one. That man has the key, the man in your dream. When he gives it to you, take it, and blow the damn thing up."

Steven was dying; I heard it in his breath, saw it in his eyes. He squeezed my hand. He'd be dead by morning.

"I'm glad you're in your own bed," I said. "Is Julia here?"

"In the next room ... she'll be okay. She's dancing."

"You and my father are responsible for this, aren't you? How long have you been planning it?"

"I knew it was coming. I cashed out on everything."

"How in God's name did you know this would happen unless it was your virus? Yours and my father's."

"I have the gift of prophesy, son. I know things, seen it all, decades of it, seen it grow. I recognized it before anyone else. That's what I do, analyze the culture while I'm sifting flour. That's what they pay me for, sweet lies. It's there … truth, just find it. You'll see for yourself in Pindar Corners. It will all come to light."

"I'll go there, Steven. Me, the children, Adina, we'll all go. It will take me a few days to get things in order. We'll take Julia, I'm sure you want her with us?"

"Couldn't stay here anyway," he said. "Nothing in Manhattan but the poor and the rats."

"Steven, was the virus yours? Yours and my father's? Tell me. Why the hell won't you give me a straight answer?"

He grabbed me by the collar. He wasn't as weak as he looked.

"Not every virus will kill you, Harry."

CHAPTER FOURTEEN

Adina

Daddy left us his van, the house in Pindar Corners and several billion dollars in cash, most of which was safely tucked away in a fireproof safe above the fireplace. A safe in the master bedroom contained more cash and valuables but in the basement of the house was the largest safe of all. It contained priceless cookbooks, including a copy of *The Big Fat Duck Cookbook* and *The Dom Perignon Cookbook*.

Daddy also left Harry all his culinary appliances – his mixers, blenders, and his Artisan Ruffled Pie Dish, not to mention his personal embosser, round foil labels, perforated French bread pans, pasta machine and a very high end set of cooking knives. We received all the china, the glassware, his Veggie chop, tablecloths and napkins, and several boxes of his own menus, all in the basement as if waiting for us.

Aside from everything else, we were happy to have the van. Daddy had used it for special catering parties; I don't know how we would have gotten out of Manhattan without it. The Zippie barely had room for our children, so we had to leave it behind. We weren't taking any of our furniture, only personal items, and of course, Harry's kitchen paraphernalia, which included ten boxes from Daddy.

We received notice from The Brain that if we did not pay the balance due on our apartment's value, we would have to vacate the premises in thirty days. This was preposterous, of course; all real estate in Manhattan was worthless. It would, apparently, be claimed back by The Brain and resold to foreign investors, most likely from the Middle East, Asia, Canada, and Australia.

Pindar Corners was one hundred and fifty miles from Manhattan. The van would not have to be recharged until we arrived, providing we didn't hit traffic, which wasn't likely. Without cash, the entire country was broke. People were already building tents in Central Park and planting vegetables for the following spring on what I assume they considered their back yards. The Brain used loudspeakers to enact the Order Law and sent out police in high boots and guns to enforce it. Simply put, looting, rioting and disorderly conduct was against the law and offenders would be shot on sight. Our right to carry firearms during what The Brain referred to as this "Fiscal Crisis," was revoked and people were mandated to turn weapons into local police stations.

I barely had time to mourn my father's death. We had to get out of the city before barriers were put up to stop us and before it became illegal to cross a bridge. But I would not leave without the families of my students. They would die if they remained in Manhattan, either from starvation or from violence, unless we helped them to escape.

"Adina, you can't be serious?" Harry looked at me with the same expression he'd had on his face the day I told him I was pregnant with Teddy.

"The house sits on hundreds of acres, Harry. We don't need all that land."

"Well, perhaps we do. Maybe we'll have to grow corn,

milk cows, kill chickens … I don't know, Adina. We have to think of ourselves."

"I will not leave them here to rot, Harry."

"No, of course not."

Harry looked defeated. I went to him and took him in my arms. "What kind of people would we be if we left the children behind?"

"Smart?"

I stepped away and laughed. I assumed he was kidding. I loved that about Harry; he could always make me laugh, even in a crisis. "I'm going to call each one of my student's families and see if they have a way of getting up there," I told him.

"And if they don't?"

"We'll drive back and forth, transport them all if we have to."

Harry started pacing. When he stopped, he ran his hands through his hair and looked at me. He shook his head slowly. "Where will they live?" he asked.

"We'll give each family three acres of land, at the very least, and build them houses. We'll all farm together for food, we'll help each other out."

I went to the phone as Harry went to the kitchen. "Maybe I'll find a sous chef among them," he called out. That was Harry; his heart was immense, sort of like Daddy's.

01.001.11.001.1.011.111.01.1.0001.001.1.011.1.11.01.1.001.0001.111.1.001.001.001.1.11.011.1.001.1.001.0000001.01.001.001.1.011.1.1.01.1.00001.01.1.001.00

It took only two trips back and forth to get the families up to Pindar Corners. We drove with our hearts in our mouths, fearing we might be stopped and ordered to return to the city. If that were the case, none of us would have survived. We took the highways even though we might have been spotted by one of the many cameras which seemed to follow our movements, but Harry said the police were too busy patrolling the backroads and shooting and rounding up all those poor souls who decided to travel on foot.

On the first trip, Harry's parents and my mother came with us. We piled everyone inside Daddy's van. The children sat on Harry's boxes quite comfortably. I told Edward's father how to access our Zippie and he drove up to Pindar Corners in it with his wife and son. Harry made one trip back and forth for the twins, their two other siblings, their dog, Max, and their parents. I came back in for Sara. Sam's father had a Zippie sedan and drove up separately with his son.

Bertram and his father were another issue.

I hadn't heard from Larry Reid since the day after the crash. We'd agreed that they would drive up at least by the end of the week. When they hadn't arrived, I worried that they wouldn't ever be able to get out. I called him, hoping he would pick up.

"Adina?"

"Yes, where are you?" I asked him.

"It's Bertram, I can't find him."

I put my iMini down and looked up at the sky. Bertram didn't want to leave the city, even with all the devastation. Things had happened so quickly that I hadn't had a chance to speak with him. Now, he had taken off.

"Do you have any idea where he might have gone?"

"No. The tunnels and bridges are guarded now. No one can leave Manhattan. You were so lucky to get out. I think they want to rebuild and put people back to work as quickly as possible. If it takes too long and people die of starvation, who cares? What's it to them? They're trying to prevent an exodus out of here." I heard the sigh that escaped from him. "We'll never make it."

"Look, there must be a way. The river is mostly dry and there are places you'll be able to cross at night. Please try."

"We could be shot," he said. "Can I really put my son in that kind of danger, even if I do find him?"

"You must," I said. "You'll both be in danger of starving if you don't. For God's sake, Larry, someone might even kill you for the belt that holds up your pants, or for the shirt on your son's back."

When he hung up, I knew he felt entirely defeated and hopeless, but I prayed that once Bertram got some sense of life on the streets, he'd return to his father.

CHAPTER FIFTEEN

As Adina and I turned onto Robin's Nest Road at the Corners for the very first time, my anxiety left me. Strangely enough, Pindar Corners lifted the burden of despair. But, as we approached the house, I was disappointed to see it in such disrepair.

"Oh, shit," I said.

"Ditto." Adina looked at me and raised her eyes.

"Do you think it has working plumbing?" I asked and wondered what we'd do without toilets.

"Well, at least there's a creek behind the house for bathing," Adina said.

"Well," my father replied, "there's nothing like the tickle of grass on your bare ass."

At least we all had a chuckle over that.

01.001.1.1.001.1.01.1.1.1.01.1.0001.001.1.01.1.1.1.01.1.001.0001.1.1.001.001.001.1.1.01.1.1.001.1.001.0000001.01.001.001.1.01.1.1.1.01.1.00001.01.1.001.00

The air was clear in Pindar Corners. It was the first thing I noticed. It hit me like a splash of cold water.

"Smell that?" I asked my father, at least a dozen times. I couldn't get over it.

"Smell is a very new sense, Harry, one I never knew I didn't have."

"Smell that, Adina. What is it?" I asked my wife, picking up a new sweet scent that drugged me with its freshness. It smelled so delicious it made me feel hungry.

"Wisteria."

"Ah, Adina, to smell is to live well, don't you think?" I reached out my arms and threw my head back.

"Yes, Harry, we have air and water. We have land and life. All is well."

We would soon discover how well when we found the wine cellar.

"Ah, yes, and a wonderful wine cellar. All is well, indeed," I remarked as I studied the bottles. The cellar was filled with the finest French grapes, not to mention some excellent wines from Oregon and Washington State, and of course, cases of Italian reds, and even the absolute best whites from Hungary. Leave it to my father-in-law.

"No house of my father's would be complete without a wine cellar," Adina said.

"Fine man, your father, fine man," I said.

It appeared that Steven had assured us a wine cellar and a perfectly spectacular flower garden, but little else about the house was in as perfect shape.

"What are we going to do with this eyesore? Even the roof slopes," Adina asked, as we stared at it the next morning.

It was a good-sized Colonial, a Center Hall. There was an old elegance to it, and I must say, it had a beckoning appeal, despite its problems.

At least it was summer. I knew we could find some makeshift way to give the other families shelter until the houses were built and ours repaired.

On the bright side, the old Colonial was large and comfortable. We had a working fireplace in the living room that I set out to painstakingly restore. The kitchen was huge and let in the sunlight, but unfortunately, the appliances were antiquated. I made a mental note to begin that renovation immediately.

And I did, the very next day. For the time being, I had a family of twenty to cook for and I needed the best stove on the market. It would have to be a Wolf, a large one. Aside from everything else, Steven had left me all his prize menus and had written in bold, large letters across the folder they came in: **To be followed to a T, Harry. Please, do not over-salt!!!!!**

I was eager to test them all but grateful that Steven would never know if I substituted one herb for another, or canned sauce for the real thing. Well, that is, unless you believe that spirits are around you, which at the time I didn't. But one night, I used a package of dried onion soup in my sauce and the damn pot went flying to the floor. Adina said it was our pet cat, Lulu, but why then, did I find two nice round onions on my chopping block when I turned?

I was sad that Steven wasn't there to appreciate a house I was quite sure he had loved, though he'd never spoken of it. Many nights I'd swear he was sitting beside me as I stared out at the mountains. I wasn't familiar with mountains. They reminded me of my wife's breasts, peaked and beautiful. At night I could appreciate the stars. I'd never seen stars before either and I was mesmerized by the nightly show of glitter and the serene and magical slant of the moon.

"Did you know he owned this beautiful place?" I asked my wife.

She shook her head. "No," she said. "There must have been a reason he never told us about it. Perhaps he feared it would be confiscated by The Brain, so he kept it undercover."

"Strange man, your father," I replied.

Steven had recently replaced the heating system and the wiring, but unfortunately, didn't get around to the roof. We found some roofing people in town who were happy to get the extra work, so we hired them. We were also able to find contractors and electricians and anyone else we needed to get the houses up for the other families.

Everybody pitched in, and I'd never had so much fun in my life. Putting up a house with your bare hands was better than racing old Fords, copulating to Rat Kill, or surfing the net with The Brain's new MagnoSoft Super Sonic Netscape.

01001110011011111011100010011011111011001000111100100100111101110011001000000101001001101111011100001011001100

We painted our house white with blue trim, and then, we all took on the arduous task of repairing the beautiful old bordered wooden floors plank by plank.

When we were through with the restorations, which took the whole summer, our old Colonial was happy; we could feel that it was happy. It smiled at me as I drove by, and no, I am not crazy, it did smile. The windows were paned and reminded me of eyes. I loved to go out at night and look back in, to see Adina in the living room with the children, through the lace. It was the most wonderful sight in the world to me, seeing my family through lace.

Our gardens were lively and colorful, and the old oak held a swing for our children. The dogs we adopted played and frolicked on the front lawn and Lulu fished in the creek. A white horse fence and two weeping willow trees on each side of the yard idyllically framed our beautiful house. Adina referred to our home as "Old world charming." I referred to it as "Salvation."

01001110011011111011100010011011111011001000111100100100111101110011001000000101001001101111011100001011001100

I found a smaller farmhouse on Spruce Road for my parents and they transformed after moving in. Mother adopted a Golden Lab from a litter and became the World's Best Mom to it; certainly, as good as she'd been to me. Father found himself a hobby: Horseshoe. He became rather obsessed with the game. Everyone who passed by the road got roped in to Horseshoe with my father.

The other houses were going up quickly and we knew that everyone would have shelter by the end of autumn. I liked the other families and we all got to be friends. The children came often to our house and played with Teddy and Lindsey. Adina still taught them on Saturday mornings. We even found a piano for Edward in a bar that had been abandoned years ago. Held together by the spit and ash of old cowboys, and nothing else, and a breath away from crumbling to the ground, it made beautiful music and we heard Edward playing for hours, his songs so hopeful. If I could dip into the old files, I'd say Edward's music spoke to our souls.

Adina's mother lived with us in a separate wing of our house. She mourned Steven terribly and said little. She danced alone as the sun rose each morning. Our daughter used to watch her through the fog. Soon, Lindsey joined her in the morning mist and the two twirled in the auroral stillness, like ghosts seeking a heaven.

Our neighbors were all amiable, helpful people who mostly farmed, ran the general stores, the banks, restaurants and schools. They thought of themselves as poor, but they had no idea how well off they were. Their children went to institutions where real teachers taught. Inside the institutions there were several schools. Adina and I visited one of them and were surprisingly impressed. We immediately enrolled Teddy at Pindar Corners Elementary. On his first day, we were met by a ruddy-faced woman who told us she would be Teddy's teacher. Under her arm, she had a copy of *A Pirates' Tale*, and in the classroom was a flag, a map of the United States, and several bookcases of colorful children's blocks.

"This is the way it used to be," Adina said tearfully.

010011100110110111011011000100110111110110010001111001001001001110110110010011001001000001010010011011111011100001101100100

My children were like butterflies let out of a jar, but it wasn't so easy for me; I had to learn how to live freely, as children do. There's no way to reprogram yourself once you've been a Computer Project baby, though it is at least possible, if your soul file has been kept on the *Âme* website, precisely where my children's files were now being saved.

We logged onto *Âme* to receive real news and soon learned that The Brain was recuperating and getting stronger every day, but as long as we were safe, we didn't care. The Brain didn't know we were rich, and therefore had no interest in where we lived or what we did. There wasn't any transportation allowed between Manhattan and points north in New York, which also made us safe from looters. If needed, however, we had all managed to escape with guns.

The townspeople gave the impression they were untouched by what had happened in the city; we kept a close watch on our neighbor's children despite that. The Brain was insidious, and now that it had imploded economically, there was no telling what it would do to recoup the losses.

One year passed, then two, without incident, and we felt completely overlooked by whatever malignant manifestation was running the rest of the world. Adina and I had a wonderful extended family. We grew vegetables together and my culinary expertise took on a whole new creative expansion. Steven would have been proud of me.

We gave dinner parties at least once a month, served fresh meat and the most delicious tomatoes and corn. The cucumbers were so magnificent I carried them around with me and ate them like mints. Our herb garden was so fresh I could smell my parsley, and basil, as I turned up the drive. I was a supremely euphoric man and there were even times when I wished Steven could see us, cultivating our land, and travailing over the glorious mountain curves, on foot, just to marvel at vistas, because we had the time to do so. We reveled in landscapes that took our breath away, and we made love under the sky, so close it appeared like a blanket over us.

Three years passed, then four, without incident, but all that was soon to change. I was in the hammock the first time I noticed the car and Edward's father walking toward me. Gilbert and his son took daily walks and always passed our house, so it was not unusual; it was the car that was unusual.

"Hey, Harry," he called as he flopped on the hammock and I nearly took a tumble. "Notice that car?"

"The black gas guzzler? Yeah."

"Thought they were outlawed."

"Some old-timers up here still have them, not too unusual to see one."

"It came from Nobody's Road," he said.

I sat up in the hammock and the two of us rocked back and forth.

"Nothing there," I said.

"Nothing but some sort of storage unit."

"Oh, that ugly thing," I laughed. Adina and I had hiked up Nobody's Road a few weeks after we arrived in Pindar Corners. Just curiosity. The road was narrow and hard to maneuver, but surprisingly, it fanned out into a large meadow, which was quite spectacular. Unfortunately, right in the center of this beautiful meadow sat this horrible concrete storage unit. We figured somebody with absolutely no eye for the aesthetic had it built for his motorcycles or tractors, or whatever.

After that morning, we saw the car quite regularly. It turned off Nobody's Road onto Robin's Nest and then did a U-turn right in front of our house before going back to the Corners and turning left toward New York City. The windows were those dark shady things you can't see through, so we had no idea who was driving. After a while, I barely paid it any mind.

CHAPTER SIXTEEN

Adina

It was almost at the end of our second year in Pindar Corners. I was in my garden and the dogs were lying in the sun. Harry had gone to play Horseshoe with his father. I had just finished planting new geraniums, red for color, against the vibrant Golden Spirit shrub.

I stood up and grabbed the hose nearby: it was early morning and it would be another dry day. I happened to look up, feeling a new presence in the yard.

"And who are you?" I asked with a laugh. A very spirited spaniel had rousted my labradors from sleep.

"Adina?"

I heard the call and turned. Way down by the road, I saw two figures, almost the same height, walking toward me. But one was clearly younger. I met them midway on our front lawn.

"Adina?" he said again.

I recognized Larry, despite his heavy beard, though he looked haggard . It took some time to comprehend this new

Bertram, scowling and lacking any recognition of me.

"Bertram?" I whispered. I wanted to hold him, hug him to me, but I was sure to be rejected. I found Larry's expression defeated and forlorn, though he attempted to smile.

"We walked all the way." He shrugged his shoulders and looked at his son, who stared at me as if I were an enemy. "We stayed with a family in Kingston for awhile. They put us up."

"Thank God you're finally here," I said.

I led them into the kitchen and while I cooked up some breakfast, I learned of their long travail out of Manhattan and up through the woods of New York State.

"We were on foot the whole way," Larry said. He drank the iced tea I had given him in one long thirsty swallow. Bertram remained quiet and barely ate the toast I'd made.

Larry put his glass down and I gave him a refill. "We survived off the kindness of strangers," he said. "People took us in, fed us."

"You've been walking essentially for two years?" Their clothes were old but clean, and their shoes must have been replaced with someone's old cast-offs because they didn't match.

"Well, we stayed with people long enough to catch our breath."

"I'm relieved at the kindness of strangers."

"My Zippie was stolen. Everything in Manhattan is up for grabs. Foreigners are buying up the real estate, so no one has a place to live, unless they break in somewhere."

"And risk being shot," Bertram finally said, his first words since he'd arrived.

Then Larry told me about having to kill one of the guards who found them crossing the river.

"I have his gun," Larry said and patted his side.

"Where did you finally find your son?" I asked

126

"He'd broken into a department store, slept in the beds, used the public toilets and ate the food. He came back to me when the food ran out."

"Is that your dog?" I asked Bertram.

"Sure," he said.

"He's been with us from the beginning, he's Bertram's dog," Larry told me.

"What's his name?" I asked the boy, who was now a very tall twelve-year-old.

"Who cares what his name is?" he said.

I looked at Larry, who gave me a very perplexed frown.

Will you teach him again?" he asked me. "He's had no education at all since we left. I try, but I was raised on Computer ... what the hell do I know aside from being a chemist?"

"Of course," I said.

I explained they had a house and land that we'd been saving for them. Larry put his head down and cried like a baby, while Bertram looked on stoically. He had obviously fallen back on the defenses of his earlier Computer Project Education and I wondered if there was anything I could do with him.

Harry came in on the tail end of breakfast and eyed Bertram suspiciously when he jumped up from his chair.

We'd framed Harry's cartoon character Mandero and hung it on the kitchen wall. I'd always liked it because it was the early version of Mandero. Harry had explained how The Brain had altered his original concept with something much more sinister.

"*Wham*," Bertram yelled and his arm went out like a weapon. "I kill you, Galactigo. Drop."

Harry stared at him in amazement. "No, Bertram, Mandero doesn't die. He's here to save us."

"Die, creep, die."

Bertram's father reached for his hand. His son's face was

127

contorted with rage.

"I'll drive you to your new house, Bertram, how's that?" I said.

Larry looked at me apologetically as I led them out. When I caught Harry's eye, his brow was furrowed, the way it gets when he's about to tell me something I don't want to hear.

Later that evening, we argued.

"The dog can stay, and Larry Reid can stay, but I'm afraid of the boy, Adina." Harry was adamant, his mouth tighter than I'd ever seen it.

"He'll be fine," I said, though I wasn't sure.

"He cannot play with our children. He's off-limits until you assure me any damage has been reversed."

Harry was right. The boy, who had made so much progress in my class, had retreated into the mindless indifference of all the other drones that prowled Manhattan.

"We'll do our best for him," I said. "What else can we do?"

CHAPTER SEVENTEEN

The Brain assures Computer Project children that the information they receive, is the only known reality there is. Our idyllic existence in Pindar Corners was absent from anyone else's knowledge. In Pindar Corners, the reality reflected had all the color and form of an endless history that would evolve in the right direction. Ages in time, when laughter and love were not searched and deleted, ages in time when sex was not found in virtual reality chat rooms, and companionship not downloadable. Ecstatic to be rid of my past, I embraced my life like a man who'd just gotten drunk on a bottle of joy.

But don't get the idea it was easy in Pindar Corners. It wasn't. Adina and I had to constantly shatter the people we had become before we arrived here, the people we had chosen to be, based on whatever legitimate choices we found online – folders we created and believed were the best practices. Adina, at least, had more experience in the way things were outside of The Brain's influence, but even she realized the despair she lived with was an invasive cancer to fight.

We were winning, though, each day and each hour

removed from The Brain, we became more and more ourselves, under the influence of nothing that would seek to destroy our souls.

The city dwellers lost everything they had, just as we would have done if not for Steven. People hungry for food in Manhattan killed for a place to sleep. My family and I might have been among them, scavenging for survival, easy prey for killers, rapists and men brought to madness by desperation.

If society blamed The Brain for all the misfortune, it was not recorded or spoken aloud. Society relied on The Brain's help; thus no one would revolt against it or blame it. People lay in wait to be saved. They lay in wait to rebuild the only society they knew. Wealth would come in greater numbers they told each other. Wealth would flow from the skies into their pockets and their digitized portfolios. Markets would sizzle and Zippies would speed through the streets on their wheels of wonder. Companies would once again consume the blood of well-intentioned soldiers and own the time it took and didn't take. Technology would heal the sick and the dying, blessed by the farewell clicks of a keyboard funeral.

There is no Brain in Pindar Corners that I am aware of. There are few towers for online connections that I can see. Our house has the only computer, as far as I know. Mostly, we live the way it was: by simple communication and pen and paper. I had to learn what it was like to make my own choices. Sometimes it felt like being reborn.

Back in the city there was so much loss; one by one by one, it all diminished. If only someone had noticed how big The Brain had gotten over the years, a hundred years ago or even fifty. That was the problem; no one noticed. No one cared about what was missing. But one thing I learned from my Computer Project Education: what is so idolized will reemerge stronger, harder to destroy, more omniscient than the God we once believed in. You do remember God, don't you? The creation of old-fashioned hope, the creation of old, unsophisticated minds? God, as we felt it, before The Brain terminated it.

CHAPTER EIGHTEEN

Adina

I awoke early and put on my sweats. Harry snored softly. I tried not to wake him as I dressed.

Outside, the grass beneath my sneakers was damp and my footsteps made soggy sounds. The sky was attempting to smile, full and blue beyond the quiet grey of dawn. The fog softened my spirits. My skin glistened. I fell into enchantment as I walked under the wings of herons and the sudden emergence of the sun, teasing and beguiling, colors that quietly spread over the sky and said hello, unabashed, not shy, forcing me to smile back.

I am blessed. I have been here nearly eight years. I live in a peaceful place where time passes so slowly my youth remains, dancing before me unnoticed. I see colors I've never seen before, intensely reaching toward me, showing off their splendor like children with secrets behind their hands, and in their hearts, and on the tips of their lips, spilling out.

I walk the same road every morning because it shields

me like a forest and then kicks me out to marvel at land that seeps and sways and never ends. It's called Nobody's Road because nobody lives on it. When I move past trees and stones and sticks to follow the path to the open meadow, I am alone. I am alone, except for a large concrete unit that sits at the start of my vista, a prison with covered windows. I put it behind me. I use the back of it to prop myself up and it threatens to swell behind me, capable of swallowing the earth. I don't know what it is, only that I don't like it.

I have never seen another soul on Nobody's Road. Harry tells me that a few years ago, a car showed up that drives here, remains a while and drives back. I heard that car this morning as I sat by the concrete wall, looking out where the land rushes slowly ahead, going nowhere.

I chose to remain behind the concrete unit as the car came to a stop. I peeked out from behind the wall. Who would come here, I wondered. I was certainly curious. A man stepped out of the car. A man I knew and have seen before. He was skinny, his back arched in a hump. He came out of the car with a key in his hand. I watched as he opened the door to the concrete unit. He went inside like a snake. He slithered inside and the door shut behind him with a slam.

I couldn't wait to tell Harry it was Crater I saw. Crater, the robot? How could that be?

I snuck away, back down the hill, quietly and quickly taking the path through the forest. When I got to the blinking turn light at Pindar Corners, I heard a shot. I ducked behind a tree. I heard another shot. After waiting an interminably long time, I emerged, my hands still shaking. What I felt made me so frightened that I ran into branches and my skin bled from the brittle and jagged edges as I found my way home.

"It's Bertram," Harry said as I ran through the door.

"What?" I felt faint enough to fall.

"He shot Edward, right through the heart," he said.

I dropped to my knees.

"Where is Bertram?" I whispered. "My God, he could kill us all."

Harry took me in his arms, held me tightly.

"Larry shot him," he said. "He's dead. It had to be done, Adina. The child was a monster."

And that was the last morning of enchantment. My heaven faded back behind the grey moan of dawn. The colors of the sun never bright enough again to tease me into chasing my youth behind trees of dying leaves.

PART II:

THE
ENLIGHTENED

CHAPTER NINETEEN

I opened one eye. My head felt as if I had been hit by a twentieth-century freight train. Everything was a blur. The form across the room looked like a ghost.

"Anyone there?" I asked. No words came out of my mouth. I tried again. "Anyone there?"

It was hard to remember what had happened. I'd been shot? Hard to believe.

The form stood. It looked like a puff of smoke.

I was clearly in a hospital room. The form came closer and sat on the edge of my bed.

"Where am I?" I asked. "Smells like a hospital, looks like one, too."

"Near death," the form replied. "Between worlds."

I closed my eyes again. The sound came back, the awful explosion of gunshot.

"I was shot?" I whispered.

The form materialized into a man and I saw him clearly.

"Afraid so," he said.

"Who are you?" I felt weak. I had a foul taste in my mouth. "You look familiar."

"Alexander."

"Do I know you?"

"Not really."

"You don't look like a doctor," I said.

"Oh, I certainly am not. I'm a musician."

I laughed. "A what?"

"A musician … played Woodstock."

"Woodstock, what's that?"

"Where free souls gathered once upon a time."

"You mean heaven?"

"No, I mean humanity."

"Oh, humanities. You don't look anything at all like a professor."

"I'm not a professor, I'm a musician," he said, showing frustration with me.

He wore jeans ripped at the knees. His hair hung to his shoulders, his mustache almost as long. He looked like one of those old rockers I'd seen online, on the history sites, the ones the Computer Project termed "at the root cause of twentieth-century dysfunction."

I tried to sit up. The man walked away from the bed and turned back to me as he positioned himself by the window. He was thin but well-formed, and still familiar.

"Who are you really?" I tried to rub my eyes, but couldn't move my hands.

"My name is Alexander Cordova."

"What? Are you related to my wife?" I said. "I don't recognize you."

"You will."

I got up from the bed. Movement was suddenly easy. I followed the man to the window. "I'm hallucinating, aren't I?"

"No, you're sleeping, actually."

"Don't be ridiculous. I wouldn't be able to see you if I were sleeping, unless you're in my dream."

He took me by the shoulders and turned me around.

137

"Look," he said.

I followed his eyes back to the bed. I was lying there in a deep sleep, or was it sleep at all? Was I dead?

"You told me I hadn't died."

"You're not dead, at least not yet."

"Your last name is Cordova?" I asked. "Then you're related to my wife?"

"Yep."

"How?" I stared into his face. He was young, maybe twenty-five. "She doesn't have a brother," I said.

"Look closely."

I stared in disbelief. He looked like Steven, just years younger. "Steven?"

"What? Oh, no, no, no. I'm not my son, I'm me."

"You're Steven's father?" I was totally confused.

"Yes," he said.

"Impossible," I said. "You're only twenty-five or so."

He brought me to the mirror. Bandages covered my face. I stared at my image. Something was disturbing.

"I used to like convertibles, too," he said.

"What do you mean?"

"You went over to your car. The top was down, it was a beautiful day. If you try, you might recall the sun, how it felt on your face when you looked into it? God, life is glorious. Too bad we can't hold on to it forever."

I shook my head as if to clear it. He was talking like a crazy man: Steven Cordova crazy.

"You reached for your hat and put it on, some old straw thing you favored. Had to protect your head, all that beautiful long hair. After that, nothing."

I stepped back from the bed and grabbed my heart. "I'm dead, aren't I?"

"No, no, no, you're not dead. Now I'm not going to repeat myself. You won't die for a while, really. I mean you will, but you won't. Don't sweat the small stuff, man."

"What?"

I slumped into a chair on the opposite end of the room.

"When I was young, we sang about love, melodic and sweet. We sang about peace, we sang together, you and me. I wish my son had told you that, but you would never have believed him."

"When were you a young man?"

"In 1972, I was twenty-five years old and you were thirty. That's when we met for the first time. Well, not really met."

I put my head in my hands. "I don't believe this. I've lost my mind."

"We had passion," Alexander said sadly.

"Passion?"

"You can kill it, you know. Oh, don't look so shocked. It's not your fault. The world changed in myriad ways between being Randy and being Harry, not all of them good. Music became angry once you got to Harry, people, too. Isolation, annihilation, login in for mother's milk instead of sucking on the real thing, what do you expect?"

"Why are you here? To take me to the light?"

Alexander laughed very loudly. "You are already in the light, happens in a deep sleep. That's why you see me, or I see you. I never could figure it out. Just don't walk into it, keep focused on me."

I got up and studied Alexander's features carefully. "You look like Stephen Cordova, I guess, when he was young."

"My boy was the spirit and image of me, or so I've been told."

"Adina?"

"My granddaughter ... in another time. Time is just a process, Randy."

"Randy?"

"For the moment."

I looked around. "Why isn't my wife here?" I asked.

"She can't be, she's not born yet. There's only one way to get back to her." Alexander held up a key. "Take it," he said. "You'll need it. If you're to see her again."

I reached out. "What's this?"

"A key to freedom. You're going to be a hero."

"Look, whoever you are, I live in Pindar Corners, been there eight years and I'm not going anywhere else."

I slammed the key down hard on the bedside table.

"Take care of that key." He went to the table and picked up a key ring. He twisted the key onto it.

"My children are enrolled in school there."

Alexander came back to me and looked deeply into my eyes.

"You can't kill it unless you kill it," he said.

"Are you mad?"

"No, I'm trying to get you to see where we're headed, what you have to do. Viruses spread, cancer spreads, evil spreads. Get it?"

"I want to go home."

Alexander sat down wearily. "You can't go home just yet."

"Death is confusing."

"No more so than life. You think death brings peace?"

"Obviously not."

"It's marked ... won't be hard to figure it out." He pointed to the key. "You can't miss it from the road but it's up high, flat when you get up there, though. You should recognize it. The land is beautiful. We'll write poetry under the willows, Randy. Your children will write poetry under the willows, too, just in a different time."

"My name isn't Randy." I gave him a bewildered stare.

"Afraid it is now."

"You're out of your mind." My head pounded again, a clear indication that I was very much alive.

Alexander made a big sweeping gesture and then

crashed to the floor. "Death," he said. "Just a kick back to life. You read the soul file, didn't you?"

"What the hell are you talking about?"

"Reincarnation, man. That soul file wasn't fiction."

"I want to go home. Where's Adina?"

Alexander came to me, his arms outstretched. "Spirits know more than the living. When you're deeply asleep, you can communicate with them, you know."

I felt Alexander's hug. I felt his flesh, even smelled his aftershave.

"What is she like?" he asked.

"Who?"

"Adina, my granddaughter." Alexander's face took on a glow, pink and full of warmth.

To placate him, I said, "She's independent and beautiful. I fell in love with her because she's incredibly special. If I could envision the perfect woman, she would look like Adina, speak like Adina and be completely like Adina. She is my guiding light. She's everything to me."

"What's it worth now?"

"What?"

"Your soul." Alexander went to the window again and looked out. "Observe, Harry, the world has gone mad. Just observe. You're in the 70s, boy. Enjoy the grass."

He crawled out onto the ledge.

"Wait," I cried. "I don't know what's going on, whether I'm dead or not."

"Go with the powers of observation. You'll find your way," he yelled back to me.

He stepped from the ledge, like a bird, and flew across the sky.

"I'm dreaming," I whispered. "I have to be dreaming."

CHAPTER TWENTY

The first thing I saw was hair, long silken hair, the color of lemons, daffodils, and butterflies with yellow wings, draped across my chest, brief warmth against my skin.

"Who are you?" I asked.

Still weak, but I wanted to touch her hair. I couldn't find my arms, though, no feeling in them.

The young woman sprang up, her face wet and puffy.

"Oh, my God," she said and wiped away her tears. "It's me, Christine."

I laughed weakly. "God?" I said. "You've reverted back to old English, good to hear it. Did you really say *God*?"

"Oh, Randy, let me get the doctor. Oh, my God, are you okay? I was so worried. I've been praying and chanting for hours."

"Chanting?"

"Baby, baby, baby." She kissed my cheek, my brow, my lips. "God is good."

I laughed again. "I didn't pass Him on my way." I looked around the room. "Or did I?"

"What is it, babe?"

"Where's Alexander?"

"You mean Alex?"

"Guess so."

"He went into Kingston for new guitar strings."

"No, I think he just jumped out of the window."

Her eyes widened, deep green eyes on a beautiful woman.

"Perhaps I should call the doctor … are you okay?"

"No, no, please. I'm fine."

"Alex would be here if he could, babe."

"Well, he jumped out of the window, which means he's dead actually, either that or he's walking around with a broken leg, so maybe he couldn't be here. What floor are we on?"

She went out into the hall and summoned the doctor. It was clear I had upset her. Had I been dreaming?

I turned my head to a table on my left. I saw a wallet, a watch and a keychain. None of the items were familiar. I looked at the archaic key on the chain, once used for opening locks. The phantom in my room, Alexander Cordova, had given it to me and it was real as the hand that now held it.

The doctor came in and removed the bandages from my face. Christine, the woman with the yellow hair, was holding my hand.

"Quite handsome," I heard the doctor say. "Care to observe?"

"Oh, Randy, you look fine. Oh, my God. You're good as gold."

Carefully, I took the mirror from the doctor's hand and brought it to my face. I moved it up and then down and then to the right and then to the left.

"Whatcha doing, babe?" Christine asked.

The doctor gave me a worried look. "Mr. Mandaro, don't you see yourself?"

I looked at him as if he were crazy. I must have had a terrifying expression on my face. The man in the mirror seemed to mimic it. "Mandero?"

"You look fine, see?" He put the mirror in front of my face again.

"I'm not there," I said. The reflection in the glass looked familiar.

"Well, perhaps if we reposition the mirror." He stood over my left shoulder and moved the glass until two faces stared back at me, his and someone else's.

"Well?" Christine said. "Don't you look perfect?"

The face in the mirror was not mine. The familiarity perplexed me. It was a fine face, though, a bit beat up, but still, exceptionally fine. A memory poked through: it was the movie star, the man who'd been trying to hit on my wife the first time we'd met.

The doctor stood back and glared at me.

"That's not me," I said. "Though I've seen him, don't know him, can't tell you his name ... but I've seen him."

He came over and put his hand on my brow. "I assure you I did not perform any plastic surgery. You simply had a mild concussion and a few facial scratches. I didn't even have to shave your mustache."

My immediate response was not to respond: I feared I would find myself in a loony bin. I had never had a mustache in my life.

"Where's Adina?" I asked.

The doctor looked at Christine, who shrugged her shoulders.

"I'm here to take you home, Randy. Marlene is worried sick. She told me to tell you she'd be here, but she had a closing. You know, that big house in Stanton?"

She bent down close to me and looked into my eyes. I felt a rise beneath my hospital gown. Actually, it was more than a rise; it was a sudden stand at attention. This woman was having quite an effect on me.

"Can he get dressed now, doctor?" Christine asked.

The doctor nodded. "You take it easy for a day or two. Don't go back to work though, take some time."

"Work?" I asked.

"Oh, don't worry, Doctor, school doesn't start for another three weeks."

"I'm a student?"

Christine giggled.

"Well, good. No sports, either. Doctor's orders."

He smiled at Christine and left the room.

"Hey, doc," I called. "Who shot me?"

The doctor turned abruptly and re-entered "No one shot you, Mr. Mandero. You were in a car accident."

"Mandero?"

From their expressions, it was patently clear that if I told them Mandero was the name of my graphic cartoon masterpiece, and that I was Harry Erin Cooper from the year 2048, they'd dispatch me to the insane ward.

"Oh," I said meekly. "Felt like gunshot."

The minute the doctor turned on his heels and left, Christine threw herself over me and stuck her tongue in my mouth. We kissed for a full minute before she broke away.

"Hold the thought, babe," she said as she gave my climbing-vine penis a playful tug. "But if I don't get you home soon, she'll have my head on a silver platter."

"Who'll have your head on a silver platter?"

"Marlene," she said. "Your wife?"

"Oh," I muttered. "My wife?"

145

CHAPTER TWENTY-ONE

Icouldn't believe what I was seeing. She wheeled me out to the parking lot, and I had to hold my chin before it fell off my face. The lot was filled with old gas guzzlers, huge cars with wings and chrome and insides the size of subs.

"Where the hell am I?" I asked.

Christine turned to look at me. I studied her clothes for the first time. Her jeans draped below her belly button and what I assumed was a handkerchief covered her midriff. Silver studs ran up and down the legs of her jeans.

"You okay, babe?"

"No," I said, touching my face.

She leaned down and stroked my hair. "You will be," she said. "Don't worry."

I wasn't used to hair as long as my wife's and it fell into my eyes and bothered me. I wasn't used to being over six feet tall either. I'd felt the height as I stood up.

"Can you make it to the car, or do you want to wait and I'll bring it around?"

"No, I'm fine," I said.

I watched as she led me to an old car with big fins in the back and a front so long, I could have lain down on it and still had legroom.

As she pulled out of the hospital driveway, she headed northwest on Route 28, in the direction of Pindar Corners.

"Where are we going?" I asked. The world looked ancient. There were places called drive-ins for food, little shack-like houses that sold ice cream and arrows that pointed to retreats and campgrounds.

"What the hell is a retreat?" I asked.

She giggled and tossed me a smile. "I'm taking you home but not before we make a stop."

She reached out for my leg and rubbed it. I turned and looked out of the window. I was in a fucking time warp and a woman other than Adina was giving me a hard-on.

"What's wrong, Randy?" she asked.

I turned toward her. "Randy's not my name," I said.

She laughed and turned up the radio. The music took me back to the sounds my father had played me, with melodic references to a daydreaming boy.

"You want a toke? Maybe that will clear your head." She giggled again.

I recognized the butt she handed me as marijuana.

"I want to go home, that's what I want."

"Well, that's unusual."

I remained quiet while Christine stole glances at me. Even with my eyes closed, her glances would have been palpable, but they weren't closed. They were fixated on the world around me, a colorful circus of freaks – cars the size of ships and men with ponytails.

"I'm worried about you, sweetie," she said. "You seem a bit unhinged, like you're flipping out."

"Flipping out?" I laughed. "Is that significant?"

"Flipping out … like, you know … blowing your cool."

"Blowing my cool? Flipping out?" How that was possible?

After a thirty-minute ride through this unknown galaxy,

we arrived at the familiar blinking turn light at Pindar Corners.

"Shit," I said, afraid of what I'd find. It was home, but then again, it wasn't.

But she didn't turn onto Robin's Nest; she turned onto Nobody's Road and drove straight up.

"Where are we going?"

"We're going where we go, Randy," she said and winked at me.

She stopped in the open meadow and parked. It looked different but the concrete storage unit was there, still an eyesore, but it didn't seem as big.

"Now what the hell is going on?" she insisted, peering at me.

All I could do was shake my head. Finally, I got out of the car and walked away. I heard her following behind me.

"You sure you want to know?" I asked as I turned. "You won't believe me."

"Try me."

I threw myself on the grass and lay on my back. Christine lay beside me and looked up at the sky. The air was light, and the sky was brighter than I'd ever remembered seeing it.

"I'm listening."

I told her the whole story, all about life in the future, the frigging Computer Project; I told her everything, right up until I went out jogging and got shot on Hawthorne. I'd been speaking for at least a half-hour or more. When I stopped talking, I was crying.

"You're right," she said after a very pregnant pause. "I don't believe you."

The grass met the sky way out before me, blue and green together in a lazy kiss. White clouds rolled by, soft dots, seductively sliding in and out of shapes. The yellow sun was a burst of heat. I got up and moved under a tree into the shade. I looked out at mountains that were younger than I'd ever seen them. I looked out on a world with color and form, vividly projecting a summer day like none I'd ever known.

She came up beside me; her silky hair fell past her shoulders. She wore beads and sandals with wide straps, and bracelets that sounded like music when she moved.

I put my head back and felt the sun on me. I breathed in, and the air had taste, soft and sweet like the dandelions in my hand.

"Maybe they gave you some medication?" she said.

"What's wrong with your air?" I asked. "It isn't heavy. It even has a lilt."

She looked at me strangely. "It's just air."

"It's just incredible. It's making me lightheaded."

"I think you have amnesia," she said.

"I don't need glasses," I said incredulously.

"What?"

"The planet is still healthy," I said and looked at her sadly. "Where the hell am I?"

"Pindar Corners." She reluctantly touched my arm. "Baby?"

I turned and stared at her. "What's the date?"

"It's June 18th, 1972."

"Oh, shit." I lay back on the grass. "It could be heaven, you know. It's mild, melodic, peaceful. Oh, shit."

"What drugs are you on, Randy?"

"Harry," I corrected her.

She got to her feet. I watched her sway in the breeze like a dance. I watched as she took off her tiny Band-Aid of a blouse and tossed it in my lap.

She knelt before me and took my head in her hands. I looked into her eyes: not Adina's. She was unfamiliar, totally unfamiliar.

"Oh, baby," she said as she put a nipple to my mouth. I was dreaming. I must be dreaming. She swayed under my

149

lips. She reached for my penis, no, not mine. It was Randy's penis, Randy's fucking hard-on.

"Must be the hospital drugs," I whispered as she mounted me. She was wet as a river, soft and salty, slippery as a rainwater-soaked puddle.

01001111001101110111011110001001101111011001100100100111100110011001100000010100100110111101110000010110011000

I couldn't believe what I was seeing, driving down from Nobody's Road, coming up on Old Lady Leeds' house on the right, first house on Robin's Nest, as it had always been.

"Stop the car," I said.

By the way Christine put her tongue up under her lip and gave me a harried look, she was clearly growing weary of me.

"I have to get you home, Randy," she said.

"Where's home?" I asked.

She stopped in front of Old Lady Leeds' and cut the engine. "Don't you know where you live?" she asked.

"Robin's Nest."

"Right, that's a good boy."

"Who lives here?" I repeated.

"I do, Randy." She giggled and put her hand back between my legs. Shit, I wasn't sure anymore if I hadn't made it to heaven.

"Come on, you know Marlene will kill me. I promised to take you right home."

"Marlene?"

"Your wife, Randy?"

"Oh, right." I was suddenly Randy Mandero and I had better start acting like him. She put the car in drive and headed up the road along Robin's Nest and I was looking at land where there should have been houses. The road was almost unrecognizable.

"Shit," I said, and watched, incredulous, as she drove straight to the beautiful old Colonial I lived in with Adina and our two children. I hardly waited for the car to stop. I opened the door and practically flew out. This was all some outrageous joke. "Adina!" I called as I ran up the drive. "Teddy? Lindsey?"

Christine yelled something as she drove off that I couldn't quite make out, but it sounded like "good luck." I rushed through the open door and my stomach flipped over. The house was covered in pillows. There were pillows everywhere. Instead of doors, there were curtains and beads. Instead of a computer, there was a box on top of a table with funny ears. Instead of rat-kill music coming out of it, a guy was singing about peace and giving it a chance ... or something.

"What the fu ...?"

A woman came through the curtain. Long brown hair fell to her shoulders. Her lashes were long, so long.

"Randy? How are you, babes?"

I looked into the face of a woman whose ambiguity was tangible, written on her face like words in a book.

"I'm ... I'm." A lie was called for. Even truth was dead. "Fine," I said.

She walked over and switched off the radio. The only way I knew it was a radio was from an old computer class on Early Antiques.

"I'm sorry I couldn't pick you up. Christine offered." She looked at me strangely. "I knew you wouldn't mind being picked up by Christine."

I kept my eyes on her expression: complexity as baffling as mazes that were endlessly alluring.

"Dinner?"

I shook my head. "Sure."

"Which is it?"

"What?"

"You gave me an ambivalent response. The answer should be a yes or a no. You shook your head and said 'yes.'"

"Oh."

She radiated "upset with me" and flopped, rather than walked, into the kitchen with heavy steps. I followed, still in shock. I lived in this very house. When? Almost one hundred years into the future, and yet, the damn place looked like a bad prediction on modern design.

I watched as she threw something covered in silver paper into what appeared to be an oven. "Want one?" she asked. "There's a turkey one left."

"Do you have any real food?" I asked meekly. The only way to get food in my day was to grow it or buy it from food coops. Only the poor ate processed food. That dung she was cooking was what our rats used to feed on.

"What?" Curt.

Discretion suggested I'd better not ruffle her feathers. She looked quite capable of killing me, plucking the hair from my body and putting my cut-up parts in the pan.

"So, any broken bones?" She slid another shiny covered whatever-the-hell-it-was into what appeared to be an oven.

"I'm just a bit banged up," I said.

"That's nothing new."

What the hell did she mean? Well, you want to know something, better ask.

"What do you mean by that?"

She raised her eyes. I didn't like her. Her features reminded me of a bird, with a hungry beak and movements so quick, you'd better watch your ass, or you'd wind up missing your moles.

"You're always getting banged up, Randy,"

I wasn't quite sure of the snide connotation. Was I a lady's man or a wise-ass who wound up getting knocked around by the studs at the local bar?

"How bad is the car?" she asked.

"What car?" I said.

Her expression was the epitome of "strange" and I

remembered I was supposed to have had a car accident.

"Oh, nothing a good mechanic can't fix."

"A change of scenery might do us good," she said, still giving me that "something is rotting nearby" stare.

"I'm thinking about accepting Alex's offer and moving to Tucson."

She didn't look at me when she spoke, which I guess was a good thing. I must have looked bizarre.

Adding things up in my mind, Alex was the madman from the hospital room, granddaddy to Adina. Of course, he bought the house. Almost one hundred years from now, his son will give me the deed, so who the hell was this woman? Who the hell was I?

"I can't move to Tucson," I said.

She looked at me sadly, so sadly I knew I'd broken her heart.

"Fuck you, Randy."

I took a breath. "I'm sorry," I said, but she'd buried her face in her hands. "Look …" I thought about explaining.

"Don't bother," she said, glaring at me like some unwanted bug in her sightline. "I already hate you, that's not going to change."

CHAPTER TWENTY-TWO

Alexander came over the next day looking as though he was ready to pass out cigars. He had apparently closed his deal with Marlene over the phone; she'd agreed to his offer on the house during some surreptitious phone call I was unable to eavesdrop on. Perhaps I had everything to do with her quick decision. I pretty much surmised that Randy, Marlene's bastard husband, had nothing to say about it. Marlene was selling and that was that. I assumed it had come with their marriage, on her side. Alex pretended not to know me, or I should say, the real me, even though I was giving him every hint under the sun.

"Hey, buddy," I said, not giving a damn that Marlene was in earshot. "I need to get back to 2058. I miss my wife. Can you help me?"

He looked at me as if I was an escaped loony tune. "Oh, man," he said. "Whatever you're smoking, man, I'll take some."

He laughed for a good twenty minutes while Marlene sat there and stared at me, her "good-for-nothing husband." I knew that's what she called me, because the night before, I had tried to slip into her bed, and she politely told me that good-for-nothing husbands took the guest room.

I didn't want to sleep with her anyway. I wanted to go home. I looked at Alexander despondently. "Please help," I said.

"Help with what?" Marlene interjected. "How about help with our marriage?"

"I'm not going to Tucson." I sprang up tall and gave her what I knew to be a filthy look. I didn't want to leave Pindar Corners. I felt the only way back to Adina must be here, must somehow be tied to this place. Maybe it had something to do with the key Alexander gave me when he knew who the hell he was, and who the hell I was.

Marlene stared at me as though she'd never seen me before, when in truth, I guess she hadn't.

"What the hell did I ever see in you?"

Alexander laughed. "You're a rich woman now," he said to Marlene. "You can do better, leave the rat in the trap."

"Rattrap?" I sprang up. "Is that what you're calling my house? Why this house is beautiful … that is, if you do away with these crazy furnishings."

I'd sprung into defense mode immediately, convinced he'd just insulted the very home I shared with my wife and children, which presently looked like shit, so I couldn't really blame him.

I heard Marlene stutter, "You're right, Randy, we should have done everything brown, just like you wanted. The refrigerator could have been brown, the couch, the frigging walls, the rug … even the goddamn toilet seat."

She burst into tears and left the room. I stared at Alexander, bewildered.

"Why do you treat her so badly, man?"

I shook my head. I didn't know what the hell he was talking about.

"Alex," I said slowly. "I need to get home to my wife."

He made some breathy sound and stared at me. "Fuck

man, you're such a loser. She *is* your wife."

He stood up and went to the door but not before staring back at me and shaking his head.

"Fucking loser. Grow up, Randy, will you?"

I followed him out. He walked toward Nobody's Road.

"Hey, wait up." I ran behind him. He was the one who gave me the key, so he had to be the one with the frigging answers.

"Why don't you like me?" I puffed out.

"I have an excellent reason – you're not good to women. You're an asshole."

"What?"

"That's my friend you're fucking with, Randy. Marlene and I go back. She was my first girlfriend in grade school, and we've been friends ever since. Can't put a price tag on that, asshole."

"Look, my name is Harry. You know damn well my name is Harry, Harry Cooper from the year 2058. You sent me here, Steven ... or Alexander, whatever the hell your name is. This is your disaster, all of it. I want out. I want my wife. God damn it, I want my wife."

I fell to my knees and bawled like a baby. Alexander stopped in the middle of the road and gaped at me as if I'd lost my mind.

"Hey, man, pull yourself together, man."

He helped me to my feet and put his arms around me. "Come on, man, walk with me."

"Please get me home," I wailed.

"Look, Randy, Marlene is sick," he said. "Stop thinking about yourself."

"What do you mean 'sick'?"

"She has some rheumatic condition, needs the dry air. You know that. She could die if she spends another winter here. She's frail, Randy. Shit. I hate you. You're a selfish fuck."

Once I stopped bawling and lifted my head, I saw we'd stopped at the corner of Nobody's Road.

"What the hell is the matter with you, Randy?"

"I'm sorry she's sick but I can't pretend to be someone I'm not."

The hill in front of us was high enough and steep enough to tire you out, and all around us, flowers grew. A wide path, wider than it ever was, swerved off from the road. Over the years, it must have become very overgrown, for I remembered it as being narrow.

"Come on, sit here, man," Alex said. "You all right?"

I nodded my head, exhausted. The sun shone on me and the trees all around us, hundreds of trees, provided some shade. I'd never seen so many trees.

"Wow," I said. "It doesn't look like this anymore."

"What's your game, Randy? What the hell are you talking about?"

"Your son sent me here, it must have been him, and you gave me a key. To do what with? For what purpose?"

He stared at me a good twenty minutes while I marveled at this new world, staring at innocence, a virgin world not yet raped or plundered. The greens were greener than ever, the blues so blue it almost made me weep again.

"My son sent you here?" He looked at me despondently. "Is that what you said?"

"Yes, Steven."

I watched his face suffuse with anger, or pain, I couldn't tell which. He grabbed a fistful of grass in his hand.

"Lindsey and I lost our son last year, you fucking bastard. His name would have been Steven. If you mention your crazy story again, or even my son's name again, I'll kill you."

"What?" I wanted to scream. "Steven can't be dead. He's my wife's father."

He put his hands around my neck.

"Please," I cried out. "Oh, my God, Adina. How can she be born without Steven?"

He hit me hard in the jaw, but I didn't care. He punched me in the stomach, and I fell back. His foot hit my chin and then his fist socked my other jaw. When he punched my nose, I tasted the blood.

But I didn't care, I didn't care at all. "Adina," I wept. I called her name with each strike. The last thing I remember is his body falling into mine, his sobs against my ear, his hands around my neck as we rolled down a steep incline. And his words "You son of a bitch." He said them over and over until it was almost like a lullaby. "You son of a bitch."

I fell into unconsciousness hearing it, this sad, gut-wrenching lament.

CHAPTER TWENTY-THREE

The clouds had drifted off, revealing a pale sky, beyond blue, nearly white. The air was so clean I wanted to drink it, inhale it into my chest like a wonder drug. Alexander sat under a tree, looking off.

"Hey," I said.

He turned to me slowly. "Anything broken?"

I shook my head, but I could have used a few Tylenols. I rose to my feet and looked up toward the top of the path. I'd only walked Nobody's Road a few times in all the eight years Adina and I had been in Pindar Corners. We'd made love there once. We'd had a picnic, a bottle of red wine, cheese, fruit and chocolate. She'd made chicken and potato salad and we'd spread a blanket in the sun. I wanted to see it again, that spot where my wife and I made love and she'd taken my kisses with wine on her breath and crumbs in the creases of her lips.

"Come on," he said as he stood up and started up Nobody's Road.

I followed behind him; my body ached, but I wanted to

get to the top where it opened wide and the mountains loomed like sweeping shoulders, covered in green grass, majestically still. I pushed myself upwards. It was hot, so I took off my shirt and tied it around my waist. Alexander was sweating and his hair looked like wayward strings. My scalp was wet to the touch. I heard a medley of birds and I kept looking up. Birds? They were mostly extinct by 2058. Now they flew above me with their song. It brought tears to my eyes. How had we let any of it happen, I wondered, the loss of so much?

"You come here often?" I asked when we finally reached the top. If I'd wanted to find the spot where Adina and I had made love, I wouldn't have been able to. However, it was easy to see where I'd been with Christine. I felt a sudden jab in my chest. I was an uncommitted adulterer.

"Yep, me and my guitar."

"I'm sorry about your son." I sat near him on the grass. Of course, saying that filled me with despair. Where was Adina, and would I ever find her now?

"In my world," I said, partly to change the subject, "we rarely saw birds, not at all in the city, but every now and then, up here, in Pindar Corners we'd hear them. It was the highlight of the day if you caught sight of one. We still had herons, but the eagles were gone."

Wherever I'd landed, it was beautiful. Alexander stared back at me and I took a qualified guess at what he was thinking.

"You being philosophical?" he asked.

"No, I'm telling you what the world is like about eighty years from now." I looked up at him and his face softened.

"Tell me about it, Randy."

"Well, to begin with, my name is Harry Cooper. I'd really prefer that you call me Harry."

At an affirmative nod from him, I shared my tale, all about the world I came from – The Brain, the Computer

Project – all of it. When I caught sight of his expression, he appeared spellbound.

"Reincarnation, man," he said.

"What?"

"Randy becomes Harry."

"You mean, after I died, I got reborn?"

"Yeah, man, if you ever get back there, you'll remember your other life. Not a lot of people can say that, man."

"Maybe it won't help me much now, but I know the soul file is real and everything in it is real. I guess that includes reincarnation."

"Far out," he said.

I looked at the world as it was then. "There's a mystery and a beauty and an enemy called man," Despondency enveloped me.

"But if you're here, Harry, then anything is possible, isn't it? If you're here, then you can get back there."

"Yeah, I guess so," I said.

"Really, man, really."

He was doing his best to encourage me, but I knew he felt as if he were placating a mad man.

"How did your son die?" I asked him.

"At birth," he said. "Umbilical cord got wound around his neck."

"Really sorry."

"Now you're telling me I have another son?"

I heard the skepticism in his voice but didn't attempt to dissuade him. "Yes, you and your wife have a son. His name is Steven."

"My wife's name is Lindsey," he said. "You'll meet her soon. She's the best woman I'll ever know."

This was bizarre. Steven had named my daughter after his own mother. So, how could he not be born?

"Steven named my daughter Lindsey. How could he have done that if he were never born?" My head was pounding, made worse by the inconsistencies of this strange universe.

"Impossible," Alexander said. "If Lindsey and I have another son … if we're that lucky, we're going to call him Theodore."

"What?" I jumped to my feet.

"Lindsey wants his middle name to be Steven, after his brother. But his first name will be Theodore."

If Steven had been there, I would have strangled him. He probably went by his middle name to get back into America after he was blacklisted from Europe, but his real name was Theodore Steven Cordova. So, we did name our child after him. I wondered if Adina was aware of how we'd been deceived.

"My wife has betrayed me," I said. "Teddy is my son's name, your great-grandson."

"Far out," he said.

I wanted to change the subject; what difference did any of it make now?

"In 2058, children commit fifteen murders a minute," I told him. I wondered if there was any way to steer the course of history in a different direction.

"What are you talking about?"

"Their memory deteriorates almost from the time they're born, and they don't form bonds because they don't remember loving or needing. The bonds they may have formed, they forget. Some people think it's caused environmentally, others think it's psychological because they're not really raised by parents. People work too much to raise children. Mostly, parents get an hour a day to zoom their families, spend what they call quality time over the iPads"

"What the hell is an iPad?"

"A camera, among other things."

"What's a zoom?"

162

"Hard to explain."

"You're painting a bleak picture, Randy."

"Harry."

"Look, can I just call you Mandero?"

"Sure, maybe I'll find a way to save the world," I said sarcastically.

"I think I want to commit suicide," Alex said. "That's what we come to after all this?"

"After all what?"

"Spreading the word, man. Peace and love." He turned to me. "How does it happen?"

"Some people think drugs caused it … the memory loss. That's another possibility, everything in tandem, working together, and we've got a society of mindless drones."

"Drugs? You mean like grass?"

I laughed. Marijuana was never considered a drug. It was just good stuff you could buy when you felt like it. It was all the other pharmaceuticals you had to ingest to get through the day.

"Pills," I said.

He leaned back and strummed his guitar. "I hope you're lying to me, Harry."

Then he sang a song about a woman named Suzanne. I lay back and closed my eyes, thinking about tea and oranges all the way from China.

It wasn't until he finished the song that I noticed the concrete unit again. It was much smaller than in my day, and it wasn't out in the open the way it would be by 2048, but it was there, hidden behind weeds, as if it were natural, like a rock.

"What's that?" I asked.

Alexander looked over briefly and shrugged his shoulders. "Nobody knows."

I laughed. "Nobody knows on Nobody's Road?"

"Here," he said and handed me a joint.

163

In seconds I was on a cloud, one that looked like an overfed sheep. I put my hands through its hair, so soft, too soft to hold me. I fell into the color blue and it lifted me up to an angel, whose eyes were tainted by tears.

CHAPTER TWENTY-FOUR

You can hear those gas-guzzlers a mile away. It must have been what woke me.

"You hear that?" I asked, quickly rousing myself from sleep.

Alexander was up on his knees. "Let's get out of here."

"What are you afraid of?" I looked around. Alex fanned the air and packed up his guitar.

"We're on private property … and we're smoking. Could be the sheriff, they patrol these roads," he whispered.

"So what?" I said.

"C'mon." He helped me to my feet. "I don't want to be caught with this stuff on me. We're schoolteachers, man."

"You mean it's not legal?"

He threw me behind a tree just as the old guzzler drove up and stopped in front of the storage unit. It was a Ford with wings.

Alexander and I stayed as quiet as we could; we weren't that far from the unit or the car.

"At least it's not the sheriff," he whispered.

"Who is it then?"

"What the—"

Alexander crawled forward on his stomach as the man in the car stepped out. He looked back at me, his mouth open, gawking as if he'd just seen Godzilla carry off a blonde.

"Who is it?" I asked. My view was mostly hidden by the grass and I was lying flat behind a wide oak.

"Pick your head up quickly," he said sternly, "but don't let him see you."

I raised my eyes. Holy flying megabytes! Fucking Crater was putting a key in the door of the concrete storage unit and going inside. He looked the same as he did that night at Maxwell's. This was stranger than the Psychic Reading Signs we'd passed on the highway into Pindar Corners.

Alexander grabbed me by the arm. "Let's get the hell out of here. What a frigging weirdo."

"It's Crater," I said as we ran back down the road together.

"You know him?"

Running like crazy and breathing fast, my body hurt like hell, but I didn't want to be found on Nobody's Road by Crater.

"Yeah, I know him," I huffed. "And he's an android."

"What are you talking about?"

"The last time I laid eyes on that man, Crater, was in a place called Maxwell's in the year 2048. Robots don't age, you can't kill them either, not unless you find the computer that controls them."

Alexander didn't answer me. We were off the road by this time and he was breathing heavily, running in front of me, and shaking his hands and his head at the same time. He looked back at me briefly. "Shit," was all he said until we got to the house on Robin's Nest Road.

"Shit," he repeated as he let the door slam behind him. "Shit," he said after I followed him inside. He leaned his guitar against the wall and turned back to me. "Shit," he repeated.

166

CHAPTER TWENTY-FIVE

The house that will one day be mine was filled with smoke and people and loud but melodic music. Every corner of the living room held bodies, some talking, and some sucking on pipes, passing them around until it resembled a sea of pipes, like wavy canoes were floating over tranquil waves.

I'd been living there, outside of my own universe for over twelve weeks. I didn't know if I'd ever get back to Adina and my children, but one thing for certain, I stayed away from Nobody's Road. Robots can kill you and you have extraordinarily little defense against them.

The house was packed, a celebration for Marlene's trip out west to Tucson. Alexander and his wife were to take possession of the house the following week and had offered me the guest room for as long as I needed. Alex told me that Randy was a World History Teacher at the local high school. World history? The Computer Project didn't include any references to history except as a footnote on the results of dysfunction. I had never even heard of the Vietnam War and yet it was the major topic of conversation. And the only reason I finally found out about the war was because someone shoved a protest sign in my hand, threw me on a

OLIVIA HARDY RAY

bus, and took me all the way to Washington DC just to hold the damn thing up.

I thought about the key on my keychain a lot and I searched the house to see if it opened anything at all there, but it didn't. I wondered if it might have something to do with the storage unit on Nobody's Road but running into Crater was sufficient deterrent to trying the locks on that old concrete eyesore. For all I knew, he could show up at any time and annihilate me.

The hippies around me made no sense to me, living on a cloud just big enough for one, coming down to earth just long enough to get laid. The only people I knew well were Alexander, his wife Lindsey, and Christine. Of course, they all thought I was insane, whacked out and perhaps mentally damaged by my car accident, but they tolerated me – as an asshole with a vivid imagination – and pretended to buy what I told them.

Christine came over and picked me up every time Marlene's car left the drive. It was hot sex, fast and a bit furious, similar to a luck fuck from Maxwell's but not quite as desperate. She talked about love all the time, which softened it somewhat.

01,0011.11001,1101.111.01,1.0001,001,101.111.01,1.001,0001,111.001,001.001.11.01,1.1001,1.001,0000001.01.001,001.1.01.111.01.1.00001.01.1001.00

Sitting back in a large square chair, getting lost in the music, I was thinking about Adina, of course. And wondering what she was doing and if it were at all possible for her to be doing anything at all when I now lived in 1972 and she wasn't born yet.

I had lost Alexander in the crowd of partygoers, but when I finally got up and prowled the house, I found Marlene in the kitchen gyrating against the body of a woman who looked as though she'd just put her finger into the socket of an electric outlet. The lamps were covered with paper shades, and candles danced, their tall waxy bodies melting, like sexy sculptured vaginas.

I turned around quickly and walked out of the kitchen. I figured Marlene wouldn't want me to find her with a woman, but when I heard her voice behind me, it was evident she was glad I'd seen her.

"I was just welcoming Jenny," she said, and a slow smile spread across her face, an ear of corn feeling hot butter for the first time.

"Nice welcome." I grinned.

"Want one too?" she asked.

Not quite knowing what else to say, I resorted to, "You bet."

She walked into my arms and pushed me back into the foyer. "I always feel so attracted to you when I'm stoned," she said.

About to tell her I felt the same, before I could speak, her tongue found mine. When she came up for air, I received the smoke from the joint she held in a clip, so hot it burned my lip.

"Tucson," she whispered against my cheek. "Please come."

With no option but to smile, I felt I was tipping like some happy drunk in a vat of ale. Behind me, I heard the raspy wails of freedom being just another word for nothing left to lose.

"Oh, Janice," Marlene said, singing along with the music. "That's us, baby, free in the desert of Arizona, building castles out of cactus plants."

I continued to smile and put my arms around her waist. I danced to the song about Bobby McGee and felt myself landing between her legs. I don't think Harry Erin Cooper could have ever gotten that big, but Randy was a frigging half-mile long.

Over Marlene's head and in the midst of our clothed but intensely developing dry fornication, I caught Christine's scowl. You must realize that in my day, we'd call this luck fuck, and just find a corner and get it on, but here, I guess, it was inappropriate.

I turned away from Christine and shoved poor Marlene into the wall.

"Randy!" she started giggling. "What the hell are you doing?"

Aware that I was in a time warp, a totally different culture. I stepped out of her arms and tried to think of beets; beets would get me soft.

"I got turned on," I said. "Sorry."

She pulled me back close to her. "Don't be sorry," she said and nibbled on my ear. "So, what about Tucson?"

Confused, I had no idea what she was talking about. "What about Tucson?" I guess I didn't remember she'd mentioned it.

"We'll buy a big house in the desert and I can sell real estate. Why not? Better to buy down there. It's hot."

"You're a real estate broker?"

Her reaction conveyed I'd said something absurd; a moment later, I realized I had. She went to an office every day, but I never knew what she did. She didn't talk to me when she came home, just kind of stared at me.

"Randy, we own Pindar Corners. The guy who bought up Nobody's Road wants more land. I said I'd sell off more. Hell, we've got acres and acres of land, Randy. We just sold our house to Alex and Lindsey. We're loaded, soon to be more loaded."

"What?" I tried to shake myself sane. "You can't sell any land to that cretin Crater."

"Who the hell is Crater?"

"The cretin that wants to buy more land on Nobody's Road."

"His name is Cooper, not Crater."

"Cooper ... what?" I fell back and almost landed on my ass; this couldn't be real, this couldn't possibly be real?

"I want to meet this guy," I said, drowning in fifty-foot waves of distress. The son of a bitch was using my name?

"Fine, Randy, you can meet him if you like."

"Harry."

"What?"

"My name is Harry."

She held the burning ash to my lip, but I didn't smoke it.

"You're stoned … H-a-r-r-y." She laughed loudly and fell back against me.

I almost started to cry. I wanted to be back in Adina's arms. I might have screamed out loud and gone insane for those arms, but Marlene kissed me again.

"You'll look so good in Bermuda shorts, H-a-r-r-y." She giggled again.

"I can't go to Tucson," I said. "My life is here, my wife, my kids."

"We don't have any kids … what the hell is wrong with you?"

"I'm not going to Tucson," I said sternly.

"I thought maybe you'd changed your mind. You've been home every night for weeks. That's not like you, hon."

I didn't know what to say to her. I wished I could make her feel better. "I like your company," I said, at least making the attempt.

She stepped back and looked at me like I'd gone mad. "But you never speak to me."

"Just waiting for you to talk," I said, still trying to be the nice guy I knew Randy wasn't.

"Oh, sweetheart," she said. "Then you'll move out there with me?"

"No," I said. "I can't."

"I'm going without you, Randy. I need to be healthy. I wish we could make this work, baby, but I don't think we can. You don't love me enough."

I don't love you at all, I wanted to say.

171

"You can do whatever you want, Marlene. I want you to go. I want you to live forever. But I'm not leaving Pindar Corners. I can't leave Pindar Corners."

"Then I'll go through with the divorce and you'll be stuck with a rotten teaching job in the sticks and space cadet Christine can have you, if she ever gets rid of Lead Belly Leeds, then I guess she'll be all yours."

"Leeds?" This was all too bizarre. I thought of Old Lady Leeds and shook my head, as if to clear it, as if to shake it from my neck and reapply it.

"Save your hard-on for her, asshole."

The music stopped, the smoke faded and before I knew it, Marlene went back to the woman with the wirehair.

I went for a beer. I saw Christine eyeing me through the crowd. I hadn't met her husband yet. I hadn't even seen him close, just on the porch if I rode by on weekends. He worked five towns over in a store he owned that sold cold weather clothes and jeans. So, he was never around, which is why Christine was able to get me back into bed. I kept telling her I loved my wife, the one in the future, and she just shook her head and jumped on top of me. I think Adina would have understood; it was beyond my control. It wasn't Harry Erin Cooper's penis this woman was riding; it was Randy Mandero's and his two-timing, good-for-nothing horny nature. I was just there going through the motions.

I looked back at Christine and took in the guy she was with. He had a huge gut and looked utterly unfriendly. I surmised he was Lead Belly Leeds, Christine's husband, whose real name was Warren. He wasn't bad looking, just huge. I was in a long, lean body, and Randy was tall, too, which was sort of nice, but at least two of me would fit inside one of Warren's thighs.

I turned away for one moment and when I turned back, Christine was beside me; I picked up the cologne she wore.

Christine's fingers slipped through the loop of my jeans

172

and her breasts landed on my back like firm torpedoes.

"What's with you and Marlene?" she asked.

I was a bit startled. "I thought she was my wife."

"You hate her, Randy. And she hates you, so what was with the bump and grind in the corner?"

I didn't know how to answer that. If she wanted me to bump and grind with her, I would have obliged. Bump and grind was an odd term for a luck fuck , but what the hell?

"She wants to go to Tucson," I said.

"She has to go to Tucson, she's sick, Randy."

"I'm sorry about that."

"You going?"

I shook my head. "I can't."

"That's good," she said.

I smiled at her. A part of me was still Randy and I felt like taking her to an upstairs bedroom, providing Lead Belly Warren had passed out somewhere, too incapacitated to beat the shit out of me.

"You look nice," I said.

"You, too." She giggled and grabbed my crotch. I quickly scanned for Warren. He was dancing alone in the middle of the room, too stoned to keep the beat.

"I'm pregnant, Randy," she said softly.

I almost fell over. I stared at her. My mouth fell to my feet.

"It's yours," she said.

I slid down the wall. Then I did some mental calculations.

"Do you have any other children?" I asked.

She shook her head.

Old Lady Leeds was my granddaughter? Oh, my God. Adina was not going to believe this.

"Maybe not mine," I said. "You're married."

"It's yours, Randy. I'm ten weeks pregnant. Every time I sleep with Warren, I'm protected. The beast uses condoms."

173

3

"It isn't really mine, Christine," I said. "It isn't really." But then again, I knew it was.

CHAPTER TWENTY-SIX

ADINA

I visit Harry every day, but there is no change; he remains in a coma. The doctors tell me he may come out of it, and he may not. It's been so long now, several months. I do all I can not to lose hope. I talk to him, mostly about our children, but he does not move or acknowledge in any way that he's heard me. Still, knowing Harry the way I do, if there's a way to heal, he will. If there's a way to return to me, he'll find it.

People look at me with such pity, so much so that I wish they'd try to hide it, at least. I wish they'd try to keep their compassion buried behind their good intentions. I don't want to see it. Their pity is reflective and clear and offers me nothing. It's static and I want to crack it open until it spills at my feet, transformed into a less weighted definition of grief.

I hold Harry's hand when I talk to him. Sometimes, he seems to hear me, but I'm told it's just my imagination. But when I go up to Nobody's Road and talk to God, He seems to listen. So then, how can I be sure of anything when I'm told Harry can't hear me? Does God really hear me then?

The doctors insist Harry is unconscious, immune to my suffering or his own. But when I open my heart, deep inside my soul, I can hear his listening. I hear his great effort to speak to me. That's the way people used to talk about God, that not getting any answers when you speak to Him is meaningless, not if you believe you're being heard.

Sometimes I am consumed by the grief I have to bear. I've lost my beautiful Edward. His lovely music is gone, his smile, his eyes so deeply blue. Both Cory and Bertram are dead, each of them shot by their fathers.

Carl Lansing walked into his house and saw the bodies of his wife, his daughter and his neighbor, Harry Cooper, lying in pools of blood. His son stood in the center of the room, his rifle raised toward the poor whimpering dog. Carl leapt on his son and wrestled the gun from his hands. He used it to shoot Cory five times. "I had to still the beast," he kept repeating.

Carl won't go to prison any more than Bertram's father will go to prison for killing his son. They are protected in Pindar Corners. But where is the healing from this? How does a man live with this? At times, I wonder if it is good to have found compassion, to be able to feel compassion in a world of monsters. But this I can tell you, I felt nothing at all when I heard that the boy who shot my Harry had himself been killed. I felt absolutely nothing when Bertram was killed. He had become one of those monsters, but God, how I wept for Edward. Perhaps that is how the insufferable sickness began.

At what point did the world begin to feel an absence of emotion, a fierce indifference to the madness?

People became angrier and increasingly withdrawn as more was taken from them. Atrophy settled in. Then, it was too late: all were stricken with this atrophy, this insufferable impoliteness, cruelty and entitlement. Call it what you may, but it was the very fuel from which The Brain came to power. These reactions soon personified the majority and society embraced itself, its evil self.

The Brain knew this would happen. That's why it became The Brain; it figured it out before anyone else, as if the devil had a hand around the human soul and squeezed it until its goodness was gone. The Brain waited behind its slime and took advantage of humanity's apathetic decline.

At one point in our history, the American Indian was considered savage, or so we have been told. But did the American Indian scalp his enemy for pleasure? I don't think so. Cory and Bertram killed for pleasure, just as in Harry's comic books. You want it, you take it.

The joy is going out of my life each moment that Harry does not awaken. My children feel it. I don't want to pass on the hole in my heart, or the emptiness, but I don't know how to conquer it. Perhaps I will bring them to a quiet place and talk about death, and loss as we understand it. Then my little student, Sam, can tell me, as he did the other day, that loss is only the perception of a finality, and that what comes around again is joy.

The Brain says that death is the end of life, and birth is the beginning. I say we can challenge that belief based on The Brain's inability to touch any dimension of knowing at all.

They tell me Harry is unaware of his surroundings, but his rem sleep looks busy. If I put my hand to his forehead, won't I be able to see his dreams? I try, but all that reveals is all that I cannot know ... or share.

But finally, something changed. I cannot tell if it was for better or worse. But when I touched Harry's brow this morning, his dark hair fell on my hand and something in my heart stirred. I sensed his reaction to me. It was different. I put my hand to the lid of his eye and raised it. His breathing increased, as if he were intensely aware of something. For a moment, I thought it was me, but instantly I knew it wasn't me at all.

I looked around the room and shivered at what must have disturbed him. Whatever it was slithered beside me ... and I jumped up. Whatever it was, I heard it moving in the room, unable to see it. Without doubt, Harry was feeling my fear. Something in his expression altered, giving way to rage.

Later that night, in bed, I dreamed I ran on Nobody's Road with a knife in my hand, trying to kill a snake coiled around my husband's neck. I went to its face and it spat at me. I looked into its eyes and raised my knife, but I couldn't kill it, not yet, not until it reared up to strike its final threat. It was Harry who spoke to me, who told me to wait for the most vicious strike of all, and then to kill it. How I heard him, I don't know, but I did.

The next morning, I drove up to Nobody's Road because I wanted to talk to God again, or what I think of as God. But I felt oddly out of place on Nobody's Road, as if there'd been a shift in the earth and I'd been transplanted into another place and time.

It was early in the day and the sun popped out of the sky, teasing me with a lengthy rise, and slowly sliding into view.

Restless, and caught between two worlds. I walked over to the storage unit, something I had never done before, preferring instead to ignore it. The windows had always been covered so there was nothing to see; yet some unknown compulsion led me to it. I did not need to understand my feelings, only to follow my instinct.

I stood up as far as I could on the tips of my toes but there was no way to see in. I tried the door only to find it was locked. Whatever was inside this slab of concrete was not meant to be seen.

I kept my hand on the doorknob and jiggled the lock. From under my feet, a small snake slithered, and I jumped back. It stopped moving and stared at me. For one moment, its eyes looked bizarre, like human eyes. I blinked quickly and turned my head away. It had frightened me. But when I turned back, the snake was gone, all except for its movement; I heard it slink away.

The ground below my feet rose up and I looked down at the movement I heard. I quickly stepped away. I wanted to run to my car and drive fast to escape it, but I was mesmerized. Held in a trance, unable to move. I saw it under the ground as it slithered. I watched in horror as it surfaced and coiled in front of me, its head as high as mine, its body now as thick as my two legs together. It stared at me with its human eyes and the tongue that darted from its mouth all but reached my face.

This time, I did run. I turned around and raced like lightning striking. Inside my car, I started it quickly, my foot heavy on the pedals as I sped away.

I knew who it was … I recognized his eyes.

Later that day, when I returned to Harry's side, I told him about the snake. A shift in the atmosphere intimated he was listening, though he did not move.

"Oh, Harry," I whispered. "Please wake up. It looked so human. I'd almost sw …. I'd almost swear it was another android, a creation not wholly human but almost."

CHAPTER TWENTY-SEVEN

Marlene left for Tucson and I now lived in Alex and Lindsey's guest room, cramming nightly for the history class I taught at Alexander Hamilton Middle School. Lindsey was six months pregnant and Christine was eight months along.

This was a nightmare.

Parted from my wife by nearly a century, my mistress was about to have my daughter, who would talk gardenias and roses with me over eighty years into the future, and Alex was about to taunt me further by giving birth to Theodore Steven Cordova, my wife's father, who would go by his middle name, if only to infuriate me.

I tolerated my dilemma as best I could, though I desperately fought for a way out, a way back to Adina. Of course, I assumed my answer might lie with the concrete bunker on Nobody's Road, but I wasn't going back there until certain of Crater's schedule. For now, it was erratic. He could show up at any time and might kill me if I were found there, inside that hideous eyesore, staring at what? I wish I knew.

Determined to find out, I always carried my key ring with me, just waiting for a moment of courage. That moment might never have come, especially after an encounter with the two new students who had recently enrolled in my class. I almost fainted when they walked in. Bridge and Tunnel together, except she called herself Bridget now and pretended not to know me. The hulk was unbelievably large, even as a fourteen-year-old boy. He went by the name of Anthony Tunnelli; he, too, pretended to have never seen me before. His nickname, even then, was Tunnel. To my great surprise, I seemed to be the only one around who recognized them for what they were – androids, images of no one.

I treated them with great disdain. I couldn't help myself; they were repugnant bullies whose only purpose in life, I was quite sure, was to torture me. If I ever found the computer brain behind these creatures, I would surely kill them.

One afternoon, I stayed late to correct some papers. It was always so quiet after the students had left, and I enjoyed my pleasant room with all its maps and globes. The surreal impermanence to the chalk dust caught the late sun's rays and I loved the white marks on my slacks and my fingers. Chalk was an oddity to me. Sometimes, I would get up and slap the erasures together in my hand, just to see the chalk dust rise in the air, reminding me of something I'd read in the soul file about ghosts, and how they sometimes appear, as if sketched in white dust.

I had given the students an assignment on the nature of the Holocaust and the insane mind of Adolph Hitler. The subject fascinated me for, in my time, this period in history had been relegated to the soul file as a fictional event. It was in this new education that I learned something vital about The Brain: it must have come from the same mindless void that had produced Hitler, and others like him.

In my fascination with indifference, I recognized the

birth of evil. I saw its beginning, way before Hitler, as an aberration of humanity surely created in the mind of a corrupted and treacherous madman. I asked myself whether that malignant and diseased mind could somehow sit at the controls of humanity in my generation, defiling its potential goodness with a thirst for destruction. This thing, whatever it was, fed on what it lacked, growing more powerful each century until it owned its hateful quest, as in my day, where nothing could be blessed or loved. This evil feasted on our despair.

If that's so, I thought, what does this evilness look like? What does it even resemble and how many years has it kept itself alive, producing dead minds that feed on murders and acts of unspeakable cruelty? Who sits behind The Brain, and would I recognize his face if I looked into it?

While I pondered these thoughts, Bridget and Tunnel entered my class. A shudder ran through me as they took seats before me, conscious of how they gave each other a sinister stare and bellowed something from out of their throats that resembled a laugh, but really wasn't. I was hardly in the mood for them and gave them a weak smile.

Tunnel was too big for the seat. He was not bald, as he would be in my day, but his hair was lifeless and hung down his cheeks, as if wet. His tattoos were all symbols of something or other. Most likely, in Tunnel's deranged robotic mind, they stood for some nasty cult of kitten torturers.

I had no idea if he knew who he was, but he was obviously a time traveler. That, or he'd reproduced himself too many times forward. In all honesty, I had no compulsion to question him.

"Good afternoon," I said politely. "Did you forget something?"

Bridget answered me. Her lips not yet pierced and her hair not quite blue, but her voice still sounded like too many sirens screaming.

"It never happened," she said, glaring at me.

"What never happened?" I asked.

Tunnel stood up and slammed his books on the desk. "This shit," he said, and his history book fell to the floor. "You can't teach this shit and get away with it."

"You don't know what you're talking about," Bridget shrieked, tempting me to protect my ears from severe damage.

What could I do with these fools but ignore them, get rid of them? So, I did my best. Perhaps they were not aware that they were misguided. Certainly, it was a useless quest to challenge them on their ignorance. They were, after all, children. I continued grading papers and did not acknowledge them further.

"Why do you people always abuse those who seek to do good?" Tunnel glared at me.

I couldn't believe my ears. "You're not talking about Hitler, are you?" I asked.

"Well, I'm certainly not talking about Joan of Arc, or Christ, or any other of your seven dwarfs."

"And what of Adolph Hitler?" I asked Tunnel. "Was he just a myth in time? Is that what you're saying? A myth, like Zeus and Cupid?"

Tunnel looked at me as if I'd asked a trick question. "Myth? What the hell are you talking about? Hitler was a visionary. Ethnic cleansing is necessary. What the hell did Joan of Arc do, or Christ for that matter? What did they do but pollute history with bullshit?"

I slumped into my seat. I recognized it immediately, put all the pieces together in an instant. Here was my malignancy. This huge atrocity was tainting our future as well as our past with his strange lack of intelligence. He may be alive now, but he was a product of the brain.

"I have papers to finish, if you'll excuse me?"

I looked at them; they were smiling, empty, sinister

smiles, as if I were some child caught with a hand in the cookie jar.

"You want to kill me, Mr. Mandaro?" Tunnel snarled. "You want to kill me because you don't like what I have to say?"

I heard Bridget snigger.

"Not exactly," I answered him.

"We know who you are," Bridget said. "But what do you think we are, human or something?"

This took me aback. "I recognize you, too," I said. "But I'm not happy to see you."

"Then kill me," Tunnel whispered. "You can't kill me, but you can try."

"I don't kill people," I said. "I don't even kill androids." I gave them an evil stare.

"Pansy hippie," Bridget spat at me. "I say you do."

"Here," Tunnel said and held out a snake.

I never liked snakes and I retreated into a corner of the room.

"Look in its eyes," Bridget whispered as she came up close to me. Her breath smelled like a dead animal.

Well, of course, I couldn't look in its eyes, I couldn't stand it.

But Tunnel grabbed me by the neck and forced me to my knees. He held the snake before me, and I almost fainted.

"Well, pansy hippie, are we magicians or what?" Bridget laughed and even the snake grimaced.

"You don't get it yet, moron," Tunnel said. "What is this little cutie showing you?"

My heart about to explode, I gasped for breath. There, in the snake's eyes, I saw Adina. It was like looking through a mirror. But sure enough, there was my wife. She was up on Nobody's Road and she was inside that god-awful storage unit.

"How did you do that?" I managed to get out.

"What do you see, asshole?" Tunnel growled and held me tighter by the neck.

Bridget made odd hissing sounds with her lips and ran her tongue up and down the snake's back.

"There's your wife," Tunnel said, "rewriting history, or attempting to, as you will. There's a price to pay for overstepping boundaries."

I couldn't believe what I saw as I continued to stare in its eyes. Adina was on one of the largest computers I had ever seen, and she was typing something onto a screen that I couldn't make out.

"You better get the hell out of here," I shouted. "Leave my wife alone because if you don't, you'll wish you were dead by the time I get through with you."

Tunnel shook me by the neck.

I knew what I had to do and felt for the key in my pocket. Tunnel released his hands from around my neck, but before I could take my breath, he replaced them with the snake.

I reached up for the reptile to pull it off me, but it expanded, becoming thicker and longer as it coiled around me.

Bridget and Tunnel left the room, laughing. As life was slowly taken from me, I figured it all out. If I didn't use that fucking key to get inside that piece of concrete, and if I didn't pull every frigging wire I found, I would die, and I'd never see Adina again.

Rallying the strength to put my hands around the snake's head, I squeezed with every ounce of energy in my body.

My strength all but spent, I heard a sound, as if it were hurt. I watched in astonishment as it loosened its hold on me and fell to the floor in a heap. I grabbed a desk, smashed it on top of the snake, and kept hitting it until it lay still. How many times did I hit it – nearly twenty? I fell before it and reached for its face. The snake's eyes were still open and in them I saw my wife, gasping for breath on the floor, as if she were being strangled by an unknown attacker. I screamed like a madman as I ran through the halls lashing the snake's body against the metal lockers, against the walls and the doors of the school, smashing it into the ground, and watching as it burst free from the fury with which it hit the ground.

It lay at my feet in several pieces, but its eyes were still open, and my wife was still there, screaming and writhing for help until she could scream no more, while I, helpless, wept.

CHAPTER TWENTY-EIGHT

I raced to find my car in the lot. I had to run over that thing, I had to kill its moving parts, all its moving parts but I didn't see the snake anywhere. It had disappeared. I drove at breakneck speed until I got to the blinking lights at Pindar Corners. Screeching to a stop at Alexander's house, I rushed in, grateful that his wife, Lindsey, wasn't there. Alexander lay asleep on the couch, but he leapt to his feet as I entered, fear written on his face.

Breathing heavily, my long hair had fallen out of its ponytail and frizzed about my face like a bushman's. My entire body was on fire and my sweat glands on overdrive.

"Jesus, man, what the hell is up with you?" He wiped his eyes as if waking from a nightmare.

"Come with me … quickly," I said.

"Where the hell are we going?"

"Just come with me … now!" I grabbed him by the arm and pulled him out to my car, nearly tossing him onto the passenger seat. I'd left the car running and put it into drive, and turned back toward Nobody's Road, doing about sixty.

"Hey, man, take it easy."

Alex's eyes practically popped out of his head when I

turned sharply up the hill.

"Hey," Alex shouted. "Slow down."

"Sorry," I said.

"What the hell are you doing? That weird creep might be up there. He could shoot us for trespassing, you know?"

"I can't worry about that now," I said as I stopped the car next to the concrete unit. I looked around. Everything appeared still. Birds twittered but nothing else sounded in the eerie stillness except my breathing. I inhaled deeply to ramp down the tension as I got out of the car, but my hands were still shaking.

"What the hell are we doing up here?" Alex asked.

He approached me tentatively, as if I'd lost my mind, and tempted to subdue me with a sharp punch to the jaw.

I reached in my pocket for the key. I honestly didn't know if it would work but I inserted it into the lock, and held my breath.

Alex watched in astonishment as the door opened. From the corner of my eye, I judged he was debating whether to enter. I, on the other hand, did not hesitate.

This thing was merely a rectangular bunker of about fourteen by twenty feet from the outside, but once inside it, it ran underground for miles. A light shone from far off.

"What the fu—?" Alex uttered as he stood behind me.

We were on a large landing. Below us was a huge round quagmire of wires. About thirty feet from us, was a tunnel where a light flickered on and off. An unpleasant chill shrouded us: air conditioning gone berserk.

"What the hell is this?" Alex said.

I looked below me. The wires were attached to a hard cord that seemed to have no beginning and no end. I heard a noise, like a whir, like wind, but it wasn't. The inside had air piped in from somewhere, possibly air holes.

"What the hell was that?" Alex yelled.

A flash had come from the dark tunnel. I recognized the

flash of light immediately.

"Come on," I said as I started down the platform we were on. "Follow me."

"Follow you where?"

Alex was now the one breathing hard, but being inside this grotesque bunker had relaxed me and had given me a sense of control. I knew exactly where I was. Well, at least I sort of knew where I was.

"We have to get to the keyboard," I said.

Alex's eyes rounded. "What are you talking about? This is not a fucking piano."

"Come on," I said.

Reluctantly, he followed me toward the wires. We had to take a narrow spiral stairway that took us straight down about one hundred feet. On level ground at last, the whir was louder and the flash of light closer.

"What the hell is this?" Alex walked in a circle, mesmerized by the wires, as I was, and clearly afraid to touch them.

"This, my friend," I said as I looked around. "Is an enormous server, and we are standing in the midst of a computer's hard drive."

"What the hell is a computer?"

"Follow me," I said. "We have to find the keyboard."

"Is it safe?" he asked.

"I'm not sure. But I have to find it. It's my only way back to Adina."

"Hey, man, that's your journey. I just need to get home to my pregnant wife."

"You're the one who gave me the key," I yelled. "You're the one who told me to pull all the fucking wires."

Perplexed, which of course he would be, Alex didn't remember meeting me in my hospital room as a frigging apparition.

"Please," I begged. "I need you to be here."

He looked pissed off, but agreed to stay. Instinctively, I knew we were inside the inner workings of a machine, and its monitor and keyboard must be at the other end.

The tunnel was dark, with frequent flashes of light from what I knew to be a computer screen. I hoped no one was in there but why would the screen be on if there was no one there?

It took us about ten minutes to walk through it. Horrible holographic giants guarded our way, triggered to react by fear alone. Holographs don't have sight, just the ability to detect a presence. They can be controlled if you pretend not to see them

"Ignore them," I called to Alex. "Breathe deeply and don't look at them."

"Yeah, right," Alex said.

He held on to my shirt sleeve and sang a ballad by the Beatles the whole time, to calm his fear, I'm sure.

"It's the only thing I can think of to relax me," he whispered.

The light flashed for a second only, otherwise we walked in complete darkness, with no sidewalls to guide us. For all we knew, we could have walked off a mountain. Instead, we came upon a large endless room, which went on forever, too. But it did have hundreds, possibly thousands of keyboards and monitors. None of them were on.

"What the hell is this?" Alex asked.

"These are computers," I told him. "But they're networked to a mother ship somewhere, perhaps the server we passed."

The flashes of light continued. We had light to see and it came from electricity, from power. The larger screen was visible but I didn't care about it, not if these smaller computers worked. I sat down at one and turned it on.

Alex looked around. "What the hell do they do?" he asked.

"They run our world," I said. "Not yours, not yet, but they run mine. Remember The Brain I told you about?"

Alex nodded and watched as the screen opened on a login page. He came and stood beside me.

"I think I've found his birthplace," I said.

"What are you talking about, man? Where the hell am I?"

"Shit," I said. I wished my father were there to help me with this. How could I possibly know how to log into it?

"Now what?" Alex asked.

"I can't get into it without a login."

Alex put his head down. "Guess at it," he said. "What would be logical?"

"Logical? I don't know. My father always started with admin."

Alex raised his eyes at me. "Try it."

"I still need a password."

"Try anything," Alex said.

I don't know how long we sat there trying to login. Nothing worked. I tried every conceivable password with admin, not even knowing if admin was the correct username. Finally, Alex jumped up.

"What did you call this thing a while ago?"

"The Brain?"

"Try it."

I typed it in as a username. "I need a password."

"What does 'the brain' mean?" he asked. "What is it? Try everything associated with it."

I attempted every combination of things I could link to The Brain. I typed in "Computer Project." I typed in the year the computer project educations were mandated. I typed in "The Brain" but nothing worked. I feared I'd be locked out but so far luck was with me.

"Try your name, Randy."

"Won't work." I looked at Alex despairingly. How the

191

hell would he know my password?

"Whatever, type it in."

"The Brain. Try your name as password with 'The Brain.'"

It worked. Harry Cooper had a login on The Brain's computer. My profile came up immediately.

"You've got a knack for this." I stared at the monitor. There was my photograph. The damn thing listed my parents, my school grades all the way through to my college graduation. Unfortunately, it also listed my death as the year 2058.

"Shit," I said, then had an idea. I typed over it and changed the date of my death to fifty years beyond but it kept flipping back. Frantic, I logged out and went back in as Adina Cordova. Nothing appeared on the screen.

"My God," I said.

I turned to Alex. "Log in to it and use the same password."

I was curious to see if everyone was contained in The Brain, or just the people from my generation. Something was terribly wrong, and if I couldn't rewrite Alexander's history, my wife would never be born. To my great relief, Alexander Cordova had a history within it. His password, too, was his name.

"Wow," Alex said. "Tell me we're high on some really great stuff."

I got up and went over to his screen. I scrolled though his history page. There it was, he had one son who died at childbirth, and another who lived a long life. I went back to the death certificate of his first son, Steven Cordova, and deleted it. I went back and changed his death to 2058.

I turned to Alex and smiled. "When you go home today, your son Steven will be alive."

"Don't lie to me about that, man."

"I'm not lying," I said as I went back to my own

computer.

"Let's see what happens to Randy Mandaro," I said as I brought up his name.

Alexander was looking over my shoulder. "Wow," he said as he read over the man's life. "He died in a car accident?"

I refreshed Alex's page and typed in Adina's name. I breathed again when she appeared.

"Come look at you're great-granddaughter," I said to Alex.

Alex stared at the screen. "What a knockout. She's gorgeous."

But I was searching for other information. Did Adina have a date of death? To my despair, I found it. According to this monstrous machine, Adina Cordova's death occurred in 2060. About to change it, I turned sharply when I heard the sound of something dragging across the floor, and my fingers slipped. I had typed in 2006 instead of 3006. I had to erase it, but the snake moved too quickly and had me in its mouth. I watched as Alex tried to free me, knowing he wouldn't be able to, that he'd be this monster's next meal if he didn't get the hell out of there.

"Change the date," I screamed, "to 3006."

"I'll try!"

Another snake slithered out of the tunnel. I tossed Alex the key from my pocket and watched as he caught it.

"Come back and do it. Get out of here," I yelled. He had just enough time to run from the snake, which could swallow him whole; it was that huge.

But Alex was so far into the tunnel I could no longer see him and the second snake turned its attention on to me.

I reached for the keyboard behind me. I stretched my fingers as far as I could, but I was the one being swallowed.

The next thing I remember was being inside the snake's belly, unable to breathe. I had to get out. I crawled forward until I saw its wretched tongue and forced myself toward its mouth. I grabbed the tongue in my hands and squeezed and twisted until I irritated it enough and it spat me out.

I thought I would be back inside the computer, but I was on the ground amidst traffic, honking horns, people screaming. When I opened my eyes, that ridiculous Bridget, pointed her finger at me and insisted I had almost run her over.

Run her over? Where the hell was I now?

PART III:

THE
STRANGE

CHAPTER TWENTY-NINE

As it turned out, it wasn't Bridget accusing me of running her over, it was a woman with orange spiked hair. I had mistaken her for Bridget because her face was full of silver and her nails were an odd shade of purple, like dried blood.

"Are you all right?" a voice asked me.

"Not sure," I said and tried to figure out where I was. Wherever it was, it was so loud around me I could not hear myself think. Horns, voices, varying degrees of laughter, music that could put me to sleep filled the space around me. I heard motorcars and piercing sirens I thought might devour me. I did not come from a world of sirens or moody romantic music. I came from a world of rage and frenzy, ambulances controlled by The Brain.

Most injured people were left to die in my world, especially if they were over fifty, and ambulances were silent. We recognized them by their size and their speed, for they were not Zippies, they were large enough to rival an old cruise ship and they traveled above ground on air tracks. I smelled gasoline and tar, scents teasingly familiar. But I was not home. I was somewhere else.

"Idiot girl was on her cell phone," I heard someone say.

"She wasn't looking, just walked right out between cars. I think she was texting. The poor guy couldn't have seen her."

I rubbed my head. The car had crashed into a store window and was up on the curb, the store's front window shattered, and shards of glass lay on the sidewalk and glistened in the night. I assumed it was my car though I felt discombobulated, unsure of where I was, but I remembered swerving to avoid hitting the girl. I'd been in a snake's belly before I slammed into glass. I rubbed my head. A snake's belly. Clearly a holograph. We had all sorts of holographs in 2058 but I'd never seen one of a snake. Snake holographs must have been reserved for guarding the tomb of The Brain.

"We'll get an ambulance over here right away," said a tall guy in a blue uniform with a badge on his shirt and a gun in his holster.

I'd read about the old days when policemen wore blue uniforms. "Police?" I said.

The man nodded. Well, I was getting to be an old hand at this. I kept my mouth shut the whole time the ambulance drove me to the hospital. No sense telling them I was from the year 2058 and my name was Harry Erin Cooper; they'd check me into a mental ward and I'd never be seen again.

At the hospital, they looked me over and wound up letting me go without a stitch. At least I made out better this time around. The only thing that hurt was what both the soul file and science called "heart" – and in my case, it was the soul file's definition. I mean, where was Adina and where the hell was I? And how the hell was I going to get back to her?

The officer was outside when I left the hospital, the one at the scene when whoever I was slammed into a plate-glass window to avoid some moron on a cell phone.

"The girl took off," he said.

"I guess that means she's okay?"

The policeman nodded. "Can I give you a lift

197

anywhere?"

Sure, I'd love a lift I wanted to say, but to where?

I told him I needed the air and he said they'd towed my car to a place on Twelfth Avenue.

"Not too much damage," he said, "just the front fender is kind of smashed. There's a good body shop over on Fifty-fifth and Twelfth."

"Oh, I know it," I said, but of course I didn't.

He handed me his card and I watched him drive off. There was a bench across the street. I went to it and sat. A wallet pressed against me in my back pocket; I was almost afraid to look. I just wanted to sit there all night, blink my eyes a few times, and find myself back in Pindar Corners in the right year.

I was in New York City years before I was born. I was heavier and older than Randy and quite a bit taller than Harry, but that's all I knew. All I could really think about was Adina, and how my hand had slipped on the date of her death. I had no way of knowing if Alex would make it back there to change it. He'd looked horribly frightened to me; pretty hell-bent on getting as far away from that storage unit as he could.

It was cold; my breath illuminated in the night as I breathed out. I wore an old coat, not old in terms of wear, old in terms of decades. It was a nice coat nonetheless, a caramel color, and my scarf was soft. My shoes were wing-tipped; I'd read about them once. Wing-tipped shoes always sounded nice to me. I leaned over and touched the leather. I liked them.

The watch on my wrist read 9:00 P.M. and I didn't know who the hell I was or where I lived. I had no choice but to check the wallet in my pocket.

The photograph on the driver's license shocked me. Holy shit, I was old. My hair was grey in the photo and I knew if I'd gotten up to jog, I'd have made it about a half

198

mile before winding out. The birth year on Shelby's driver's license was 1960, and he looked at least fifty years old.

Well, regardless of the damn century, my name was Shelby, last name Morton. Shelby Morton? It had a familiar ring, but I couldn't place it. Well, I guess my looks went with my name. Shelby had a nice smile, but if you saw him once, you wouldn't recognize him again. He was nondescript.

I hailed a cab to where I lived on Third Avenue and Seventy-third Street. I had no idea if I lived alone, but had no option but to find my way home. I was tired and hungry, and a bit freaked out by the cab driver, who wore a turban, burned incense in his cab and drove as if a bee had flown up his ass.

The Magi flew through the streets as I looked out of the window. Hell, The Brain didn't allow anyone with turbans on city streets. People who wore turbans were liable to be shot. Turbans, Yamahas, women in saris were all forbidden, as was any other ethnic garb. It was called the Anti-Ethnic Display Act of 2033. We all had to be Atheists, at least fifty percent Caucasian, and we all pretty much dressed alike since creativity was not permitted.

The city had a certain beauty, so I wasn't home in my own decade, though New York was my home. But the air didn't stink. As far as I could tell, I was somewhere between 1990 and 2015. That's the year I was born, 2015. I was born into what came to be known as the technological age, the turning point of technology. Technology slowly became the God we worshipped, and The Brain slipped into power. Laws became his as the environment shriveled, the freedom we prided ourselves on stolen from us. Men who lacked consciences ruled us and massive technology appeared out of nowhere for the good of the people, touted as the "New World in Digital Innovations."

It wasn't known at first what those innovations were exactly, but they later proved to cover every aspect of society, starting with transportation, financial markets, information systems and political platforms, and of course, education.

As I got out of the cab in front of one of those strange geometric buildings that had probably gone up in the 1980s, I grabbed a newspaper before going upstairs. From what little I could remember of history, I appeared to be in a time later than the eighties because of the bimbo's cell phone, the way it was shaped, like the old iPhones. The Magi had kept talking into his and practically everyone on the street walked around talking to their phones with their antiquated blue tooth technology, or what I assumed to be blue tooth earbuds stuck in their ear. Maybe this is where it started, this indifference to the rest of the world.

"Good evening, Mr. Morton," said a guy in a grey suit as I walked past. I checked out the date on the paper as the elevator deposited me on the twenty-third floor: 2003. The New York Times was extinct in my day, but I'd heard of it. We didn't have newspapers, just technology that gave us news as relevant as the latest razors for pubic hair and cupcake recipes devoid of sugar.

Some quick calculations as I used the old key to let myself in meant Alexander Cordova was somewhere in his sixties by now and his son, Steven, was a grown man in his mid-thirties. I had to find him. Adina wouldn't be born until 2018. Steven told me he was quite a ladies' man and didn't marry Julia until his late thirties, which meant I had time. He was somewhere in this city.

Something inside my head screamed: where's Adina, how could I exist in a place that didn't know her name? But then again, I had existed in 1972. I had found The Brain long before he came to power and he lived in Pindar Corners. How odd.

01001110011101111011000100110111101110011001000111001001001110110011001000000101001001101111011000101001100

Shelby's apartment was a mess. He had girlie magazines

all over the floor, unfinished drinks on the table and a pile of Chinese food containers lined his fancy granite top kitchen counter. I felt like puking.

About ten windows looked out onto Manhattan from the twenty-third floor. Of course, everything looked ancient to me, but I guess, in 2003, it was considered high-tech.

Shelby's driver's license photo hadn't done him justice, he was more handsome in real life, or at least in the life he reflected from the bathroom mirror. But his eyes were heavily lined, his face ruddy, as if he walked around perpetually embarrassed. His lips turned down in an unhappy U-turn. His image upset me, and I turned away. His familiarity gnawed at me, nothing I could put my finger on.

In the living room, I looked through all his personal things. He had a photograph of himself with an attractive woman and a little girl of about ten years old on his bookcase. Old Shelby was once a good-looking guy with a winning smile. I wondered what the hell life had done to him.

I had to get up to Pindar Corners and regretted having tossed Alex the key. I should have kept it and changed the date of Adina's death myself, but who knew I'd be shot through another frigging time machine. I needed that key now, to change everything around, to save Adina, just in case Alex never went back to do it. But if I didn't get some sleep, I wouldn't be good for anything the next day except a trip to the corner bar, a recurring urge I had to have a drink, a physical impulse I was picking up from Shelby.

I found a nice silky pair of pajamas in Shelby's drawer. The guy lived like a slob, but he dressed like a millionaire, luckily for me.

Just about to doze off, the phone rang, jarring me out of a peaceful zombie state. I knocked a few things over as I reached for the phone in the dark, a big clunky thing that felt too big for my hand.

"So how was it, Shel?" a voice spoke to me, a man's voice.

How the hell was what? I thought. Instead, I said, "Swell."

"Swell? That's all you have to say?"

I stared into the darkness; what the hell else could I say?

"Jesus, Shel, it isn't every day you get nominated for a Rueben's Award."

I sat up quickly and found a lamp by my bed, which I turned on. Of course, I knew what a Rueben's Award was. I was a cartoonist, and it was still an honor to receive a nomination, much less the grand prize. Had I won it?

"Did I win?" I listened to the silence at the other end.

"Shel, have you been drinking?"

I shook my head; this was all too bizarre. "Drinking? No, no," I said as I made my way into the living room.

"Then what happened? Weren't you at the Plaza tonight?"

I picked up the photograph of Shelby and stared at his wife. Sheesh, she was familiar: who the hell was she?

"I had an accident," I said to whoever the hell I was speaking to.

I told him about the bimbo with the cell phone and that if it weren't for my seat belt, I would have been headless.

Thoughts raced through my mind a mile a minute. Shelby was a cartoonist? I suddenly remembered an aunt on my mother's side. Yes, of course, Mother's elder sister had been killed in an accident. I paced the room, to recall whatever I could about my Aunt Louisa. I rummaged frantically through Shelby's things. I finally found old mail: to Shelby and Louisa Morton. Then I remembered that Shelby was a cartoonist and had sat with me as a child as we sketched wild, bizarre figures and then named them.

I collapsed on the couch. My God, I was related to Shelby. Well, sort of, kind of, related. The young girl, their daughter, I presume, had also been killed in that accident, a plane crash. I remember the dread in our house after we received the news, the months that Mother spent depressed and even my father could not comfort her. Yes, my Aunt Louisa. I had known them. For God's sake, I had sat on Shelby's lap.

"You still there, Shel? You just disappeared. You left me hanging on for ten minutes."

"Yeah, yeah, sorry."

I finally got rid of whoever the hell I was talking to by telling him I was about to lose my dinner.

I wondered if I'd been related to Randy, too. Was this bizarre time-travel warp I'd found myself in a family curse? I looked for a computer and discovered an old laptop on Shelby's desk. I looked up Steven Cordova and found nothing. I rummaged around all sorts of yellow books and phone books and found nothing on Alexander Cordova either. I needed my car. I had to get back to Pindar Corners as quickly as possible.

CHAPTER THIRTY

The guy who called was Chip Cavanaugh, my boss at Adventure Comics. He showed up at my door and awakened me from a deep sleep the next day. The front doorbell almost gave me a heart attack as I sprang up from bed at the piercing sound, an alarm that went off inside my head instead of outside of it.

"Who is it?" I asked, peeking through the hole in the door.

"It's me, Chip, your boss, Shel. Open up."

"Oh, sorry," I said and opened the door to a wiry and nervous-looking man,

"Shel, Shel," Chip muttered as he slapped me on my back and sat me down. "I'll make the coffee. You look like shit."

I stared at him. I didn't think I'd survive another Earth walk through the time zones. I felt defeated.

"I took a flight out last night, right after we spoke. You didn't win, Shel, but you were nominated. You're a made man. That's what matters, that nomination."

"What time is it?" I asked.

"Two in the afternoon, but don't worry. Take all the time

you need. But I could use you back at your desk on Monday."

"Ever hear of a chef named Steven Cordova?" As I calculated Steven's history, I realized he'd be just starting out in his career. "My God, if Steven is only thirty, then Alex must still be alive. Shit," I said.

Chip looked at me as if I were nuts. "You okay? Who's Alex?"

"I need my car." If Alex were alive, he'd be living in Pindar Corners, must be. I could get to him. I could also get to the key and change the date of Adina's death.

"I don't think you should drive, Shel, take it easy today."

I ran into the bedroom and pulled on my clothes. "Sorry, Chip," I yelled out. "I need to be somewhere."

Chip stood in the doorway in jeans and a nice orange Izod shirt. His hair was in a buzz cut, and like the old Harry Erin Cooper, he had dimples. I had the inclination to open a box of Fruit Loops and ask him if he needed his report card signed before I sent him off to school.

"What's so important you have to rush off? I think you need to rest."

I smiled at him reassuringly. "Thanks for your concern, Chip, but I have to be somewhere. I've got a date."

"Okay." He pouted. "But we have to discuss Mandero on Monday. I'm thinking his storylines are too juvenile. We need an adult hero. There's a movie contract in the cards if we can bring a little maturity into your creation, Shel."

I was sitting on the bed, with only one sock and one shoe on but he'd stopped me dead in my tracks. *Mandero?*

"We'll talk about it," I said.

"The coffee's done, Shel."

I laced my shoe and sprang to my feet. "I don't have time," I said. "I have to be somewhere. I've got to … look, Chip, thanks, but I must get out of here. Be my guest, have the coffee. Relax. Lock up when you leave."

With that, I ran out and found a taxi on the corner.

"Police pound on Twelfth Avenue," I told the cabbie, "And step on it."

01,001110011101111011000100110111101101001000111100100110011011100110011010010010010010110111101110000010110010

I drove up to Pindar Corners with the fender tied to the front of my car with a piece of cord and prayed the potholes were minimal. By the time I pulled into Alex's driveway, the fender was kissing the ground and my accordion front end looked as if it was missing a tooth.

I ran up the drive screaming his name. "Alex, Alex," I called.

Some man who was not Alexander Cordova wandered outside, pulling up his pants. His belt flapped in the breeze and he was shirtless.

"Hey, man, it's Saturday evening. What the hell is your problem?"

"Where's Alex? Alex Cordova?" I panted like a puppy after a game of ball. "Did he move?"

He stared at me. He looked like a fifty-year-old hippie. Like the 70s hadn't left Pindar Corners. His stomach fell over in folds and his hair was grey, like mine, except his was long, too long for a corporate job.

"He's dead," he said.

"What"

He looked at me and shook his head. "He died, a snake bite, died a long time ago."

"Dead? Oh my God."

"Hey, man, just give me a minute to digest this. Who are you?"

"Did he leave a key?" As I said it, I knew it sounded ridiculous. If he died of a snake bite, then he died that day, the day we were both together in the storage bunker. Maybe he left the key somewhere in the last pair of pants he wore. I wondered how I could get away with asking for those.

"Did you know him?"

"Yeah, I knew him. Look, did he leave me a key? My name is Randy. Did he leave Randy a key?"

"To what?"

"To, to a … ah … a computer."

A woman suddenly opened the door of the farmhouse and called down to the man. His name was Luke.

"Lindsey?" I said.

She started toward me.

I felt faint. "The key," I whispered. "Did he leave you a key?" It was all too much for me and I felt myself weakening.

"Shelby?" the woman said. "What the hell are you talking about, what key?"

"You know him?" Luke said. "He said his name was Randy."

Lindsey nodded her head. "I know him," she said. I looked between her and Luke. I wondered how many strangers she was sleeping with.

"I know you?" I said to her.

"Of course. Shelby Morton, sure, you own the house on Hawthorne." She stared at my shocked expression.

"I do?" I whispered.

Luke caught me as I slipped to my knees. Alex was dead, they were all gone, and there I was, traveling through time without a map or a compass? I didn't want it. I just wanted to get back to my wife, to my life in 2058, for better or worse.

"Adina," I whispered, right before I passed out.

CHAPTER THIRTY-ONE

Adina

Harry is getting no better and they tell me I should let him go, but I can't, not yet. Not until I've exhausted every possible chance of getting him back.

"I'm going there," I told him as he lay there in a coma. "It's where the answers are. I know it."

I swear I saw him respond. A slight twitch of his body. I stared at him intently.

"Did you say something, Harry?" I put my ear against his mouth.

But he did not answer me and lay silent.

01.0011.11001.101.111.101.11001.001.101.111.101.1.001.0001.11.1.001.001.001.11.01.11.1.001.1.001.000000.101.001.001.101.111.101.1.00001.01.1.001.00

After I left the hospital, I drove up to Nobody's Road with a ladder. I'd been thinking about this for weeks. I knew I had to do it. I put the ladder against the concrete storage window. I didn't tell my children what I was going to do, I just took the car and left. I prayed nothing would happen to me, but I couldn't be sure of that.

I could barely reach the window. I took the hammer I'd

brought with me, raised it above my head, jumped as high as I could and brought the hammer down on the glass; it shattered and broke. I put on the garden gloves I had brought with me and shimmied up to look inside the concrete unit. As I brushed away the glass, I saw nothing but blackness, just a big black empty hole. I hoisted myself through the window despite that.

I hung on the inside of the unit, my legs touched nothing, and I didn't know how far I'd drop. I reached into my pocket and pulled out a quarter. I let it fall to the ground. To my enormous relief, I heard it hit bottom about a foot under me. I released my hands and let myself drop onto a landing.

As my eyes adjusted to the darkness, I made out switches, hundreds of them. I wasn't sure, but I guessed I had landed by a gigantic server. Before me was a stairway that went down. I followed it, barely able to see where I was going. All around me was a sound similar to the whir of a faraway plane.

In the distance, was a glow of lights and I heard people speaking. My eyes adjusted slowly to the light and identified hundreds of small-screen computers around me.

I crept softly forward, unsure of what I'd find: it was like an underground city and I had no idea where I was walking. Holographs in the shape of large dogs with great square jaws guarded where I needed to go.

I took another quarter from my pocket and threw it to my right. The dogs chased the sound, and I ran forward, just sliding inside a large square opening. It sucked me in as if it were a huge funnel of air. I didn't know where I was, but suddenly there was light, lots of it. It was almost too bright. The dogs returned and put their faces up to me. I tried to run, but met with glass walls all around me and I couldn't move forward.

The dogs snarled at me. Tricking them by not showing

fear would be difficult. As I took in my surroundings and ignored the dogs, another challenge manifested: I could not escape from the square room. But, thankfully, the dogs could not get in.

I was so startled that my heart stopped for a moment. A boy sat before me. His face was big and round with large ears; he had so many teeth, he couldn't close his mouth. The slits for eyes were so small, they hid the color. He typed onto a keyboard before him. I watched him intently, wondering if he knew I was there. In an instant, I was walking in a meadow. I heard the boy's laughter. He typed again and I was suddenly underwater.

I had no way to escape from the prison the boy was creating for me. God help me – I was his screensaver – my image projected on hundreds of computer screens behind the boy.

For hours, he manipulated me around and around, dragged that way and this, until he finally found a room to place me in. It had a radio which played music. The boy dragged me to a chair. He smiled such an innocent smile, as if he hadn't realized he'd entrapped me. But I was lost there, inside his computer: he could do with me whatever he chose.

I tried to speak, to plead, to beg to be freed, but he would not hear me. At one point, he went away, and I lingered in that room, but he returned after a short while, and dragged a dog to sit at my feet, and then a goldfish bowl with a bright blue fish inside it. He came back many times to change my surroundings. He listened when I spoke, but did not respond.

Is this my fate, I wondered, to be lost in eternity to this?

CHAPTER THIRTY-TWO

I woke up on Lindsey's couch, drained and weary. "Where's your son, Stephen?"

"Europe," she said. "He moves around a lot. He's a chef, studying in several different countries."

"Can you get hold of him?" I asked.

"Well, eventually. He calls home every now and then."

"It's imperative I get in touch with him. Will you tell him to get in touch with me?" I wrote Shelby's address and phone number down for her. "Tell him it's important."

I assumed I'd eventually hear from Steven and tell him about his father when I was Randy and remind him again of our relationship when I was Harry, that I'd married his daughter and survived because of him, because he'd sent me to Pindar Corners.

Sure, I thought, Steven has no memory of ever knowing me. Steven, will probably ignore a request to get in touch with me, some older man who owns a house on Hawthorne.

Despondently, I got back in my car with the drooping fender and drove up to Nobody's Road. To my horror, it had become a forest, overgrown with trees. I couldn't find the concrete storage unit: it was as though it had never existed. I ran through the forest, searching and screaming out Adina's name. I finally collapsed on the ground and wept like a baby. Everything was so overgrown, I was barely able to find the road and my car.

01.001.1.1.001.1.01.1.1.1.01.1.0001.001.1.01.1.1.1.01.1.001.0001.1.1.1.001.001.001.1.1.01.1.1.001.1.001.0000001.01.001.001.1.01.1.1.1.01.1.0000.1.01.1.001.00

I drove back to the city and went to a bar. I told everyone who would listen that I was Harry Erin Cooper from the year 2058, but of course, no one believed me, and that made me drink more.

I dragged myself into Shelby's office on Monday, an address in Flatiron I found in Shelby's apartment. I located my office among five or six others because I recognized my cartoons on the desk. I entered the room, stared at my drawings and read the copy with the sketches. Mandero was a crime fighter by night and oddly resembled Chip Cavanaugh by day. I wondered if Shelby had done that on purpose.

We were a small office, no more than nine people. I assumed we were a division of a larger parent company. We worked two comics, *Galactico* and *Mandero*. Galactico was from the planet Orion and he had superpowers. When the world was close to annihilation, you called on Galactico; when there was a lady in distress, Mandero came to her rescue.

Simple enough, I thought, not at all like the two superheroes of the future who turned evil into a sport.

My office was private and very white. Apparently, Shelby liked to play music when he worked, and a love song with a melodic swing was putting me to sleep. I switched it off and looked out of my window. Manhattan's skyline had not changed, except it was more visible. The Chrysler building loomed in the distance, one skyscraper after another not yet covered in smog. The sun bounced off the buildings, it was a hazy day, and the air conditioner was on overtime.

Shelby was sweating. His shirt stuck to my back. I

couldn't get Adina off my mind. I couldn't wrap my head around the fact that she didn't exist in the same world I did. I had to get back to Pindar Corners: I had to find that goddamn bunker, or whatever the hell it was.

"Hey, Shel."

I looked up at a man with no hair, an earring in his left ear and a body so perfect, he might have been created from someone's pen, from someone's fantasy.

"Hey," I said back, wondering who the hell he was.

"I hate to throw this at you, Shel," he said. "But Chip wants me to work on *Dark* and *Blood*, make them more sinister.

"Dark and Blood?"

"Yeah, the new cartoons?"

I almost fell off my stool. "Dark and Blood? You've got to be kidding."

"They can't be destroyed without the laser. It's the laser that can kill them. That's the catch, someone has the damn laser, a special laser, but even though they'll come close to finding it, it will evade them repeatedly. So, they're always in jeopardy. They're perfect dark superheroes. They go around killing everybody. Mandero and Galactico are too nice. Violence sells. These kids don't want nice."

"Of course," I said. Here's the beginning of my world, I thought. "What's the storyline?"

He looked at me like I'd said something ridiculous. "That's yours, Shel. I just create them graphically, from your drawings."

"Big mean ugly things, I would imagine?"

"Yeah, I think I can have some sketches for you in a couple of days."

"Sketches of what?"

"Dark and Blood," he said.

"Sure," I said. These weren't my monsters, they were created by somebody else. I just had to write the story.

He stared at me, waiting for me to say more. Finally, he turned around and left. Is this where it all started, I wondered. Am I supposed to do something with this? Have the monsters we created become real, have they become our annihilators?

I went home that evening and tore apart Shelby's apartment, looking for information on the house he owned upstate on Hawthorne Road. Eventually, I found a folder with the deed and some expense slips for work he'd had done. He'd updated the kitchen and put in a new septic.

It was late and I knew I'd never hold up for the over an hour's drive. When I awoke, I threw some clothes in a suitcase and called Chip.

"I'm not coming in today, Chip," I said. "I need some time."

"Well, sure," he said. "Take all the time you need, Shel."

I had the impression he didn't really mean what he was saying, that he was pissed I'd be taking off in the middle of introducing our new superheroes, Dark and Blood. I wondered why he wasn't letting me create the graphic for them, why he'd bring in his own artist. But I didn't have time to ponder that. I had to find the concrete storage unit, get back to that computer.

When I got to Hawthorne, it turned out Shelby owned the very house where I'd been shot by Cory. I wondered if all these coincidences meant anything, but I didn't have time to think that through. I had to find out who owned Nobody's Road now, I had to have the land cleared, had to get to the unit.

The house looked as if Shelby hadn't been there since his wife's death, but had made rare checkup visits at least. Everything was in order, so much so that the house had an eerie quality. I opened the curtains and let in the sun. I found coffee in the kitchen and made myself some. The milk had gone bad, so I drank it black.

I must have sat at the kitchen counter staring into space for at least an hour. I didn't have any thoughts in my head. I felt comatose.

I pulled myself together as best I could and drove over to Lindsey's. I was hoping Luke wouldn't be there. He gave me the creeps.

Lindsey invited me in and offered me coffee with cream, which I readily accepted. She also gave me a slice of coffee cake.

"You look like shit, Shelby," she said.

I nodded my head.

"It's been three years." She reached out and put her hand on my arm.

"What's been three years?"

She looked at me oddly. "Your wife's death?"

"Oh, I know," I said.

"Can I help?"

"Who owns Nobody's Road?" I asked.

"Why?"

Not knowing what to say, I made up some lame excuse about needing to find the owners to make an offer on the property. Lindsey looked at me as if I were out of my mind. Nobody's Road was just that, a road, and now you couldn't even call it that; it was forest, the road overgrown. It went up on one side and dropped away on the other, with a beautiful view of mountains surrounding it at the top. At least that's what it used to look like. Now it looked like a bunch of undergrowth and hundreds of trees, no beginning and no end.

"I'd go into town and ask at the real estate office," she said.

She gave me a name and I put it in my pocket and thanked her. I got a sense of her loneliness as I walked out. She'd raised her son, lost her husband and now she had nothing to do. I saw the pamphlets on the table as I walked

out, information pamphlets on the Jehovah's Witnesses.
She'd found a passion. Tremendous guilt washed through
me, as though I'd been the cause of her husband's death,
maybe. The Jehovah's Witnesses had been in the soul file,
but The Brain referred to it as bullshit; ignorance was taught
at the Computer Project and many religions were touted as
examples. They called a belief in heaven ignorance.

"Do you believe in God?" she asked as I turned to say
good-bye.

"How could I not," I answered. "If you knew my life,
you would never doubt that God is possible."

CHAPTER THIRTY-THREE

The broker negotiated the sale of Nobody's Road for a mere six thousand dollars. Jason Lloyd owned several surrounding acres, which included Nobody's Road. He'd planned to build on it, but never did and was clearly glad to be rid of it. I was happy he'd agreed to sell it: I had to purchase it. I'd been expecting to negotiate with Crater, who had owned the land in 1972 under the name of Cooper, but to my great dismay, the broker insisted that the land had belonged to Jason Lloyd's family for fifty years.

I assumed then that the part of history I had lived as Randy Mandero no longer existed, or never had. My memories existed only in my mind. That might mean they'd been wiped clean by a delete button on a computer, but I couldn't be sure of anything, so I went forward with only one mission in mind: to find Adina.

As soon as the deal went through, I hired a company to clear the land around the storage unit. They told me they hoped to find the storage unit I insisted was there and kept telling me they had found nothing, but promised they would let me know immediately if it turned up.

I went back to the city, concentrated on *Dark* and *Blood*, and what a ridiculous idea it was, while anxiously anticipating a call from the contractors telling me they'd found the unit. It had existed in my time, in 2058, so it must be there.

I also waited for Steven's call and wondered if it would ever come. I called Lindsey twice a week to find out if she'd heard from her son; he was still sending postcards from all over Europe describing his last meal in great detail, with recipes for sauces and new ways to flavor fish. He sent her the names of the wine he wanted her to track down in the city and some money to purchase a Cuisinart steamer.

The guy with no hair and the earring was Desmond Kraft. He brought me his sketches about two days after I arrived back from the Hawthorne house. I was quite sure I was hallucinating as I stared at the sketches: Bridge and Tunnel.

I looked up, a horrified expression on my face for sure. "Where did you get these sketches?"

"That bad, huh?"

"Where did you get these?" I came around the desk to meet his gaze head-on.

"They are the perfect modern monsters," he said. "Don't you think? I mean, they look like any kids out there with a weakness for orange hair and body jewelry. And one should be a woman, don't you think?"

He was pleased with himself. I scrutinized him more intently.

"These are real," I said. "I mean, they already exist. He wants us to use them as Dark and Blood?"

"How could they exist... they're caricatures?"

I perked up. "They exist. He must have seen them. Who is the artist?"

"Knute." He stared at me as if I should have known the name. "My sister's kid, Knute. He's strange but very gifted."

"He's a kid?"

He nodded.

"What does he have to do with Bridge and Tunnel? How does he know them?"

"He created them. That's what he told me. It was all his idea. He's a genius, that kid. He thought of the monsters, their indestructibility. You mean he got it from somewhere else? It sounded original."

"I'm not sure if he did or not. Can I meet him? This just may be a strange coincidence."

Desmond looked at me and shook his head. "Look, this kid has such great ideas. He's thought up this world that's run by computer. Everything and everyone, the whole goddamn government, everything. Our heroes are going to be from the future. I think Chip wants to sign him on, despite his age."

Every organ in my body froze. "Can I meet him?" I asked again.

"He's not very people-friendly," Desmond said.

I had to play this right: I walked a thin line and didn't know how much this kid, Knute, knew about my world, but I had to find out.

"He sounds fascinating… I have to meet him. How old is he?"

"Fifteen," Desmond said.

Yes, I thought, the perfect age. He grew up in the dawn of technology. He never knew a world not run by technology. Now technology is just getting more and more sophisticated, more deadly and more extensive.

"Yes, well, when can I meet him, Desmond?"

Desmond said he'd arrange it. Weak at the knees, I suspected I would be coming face to face with The Brain.

01.001.1.1.001.1.01.1.11.01.1.0001.001.1.01.1.1.1.01.1.001.1.0001.1.1.1.001.001.001.1.1.01.1.1.01.1.001.0000001.01.001.001.1.01.1.1.1.01.1.00001.01.1.001.00

We drove all the way out in Queens to a place I'd never been. It was near the water and the houses looked made of cardboard, stacked in a row about a block from the ocean.

The sound of the sea was giving me a headache; I'd never heard the ocean before – an enormous giant animal gasping for breath. But, oh, the smell was glorious. I wanted to tell Desmond to drive me farther, so I could get that euphoric scent of salt and freshness. Overcome with joy as I whiffed the air like someone with an obsessive fetish, Desmond did not understand my exuberance.

"You all right? You want me to pull over?"

"No, no," I said. "I'm just doing my morning routine before I jog. You know, breathe in, breathe out."

"You're not jogging, Shelby. You're sitting."

"Always necessary to breathe, Desmond."

He pulled up in front of a green house, not green as in emerald, more pea soup, with shutters like haphazard crackers. Had I still been exhaling, I might have blown it over.

"This is it, Shelby."

I got out of the car and took in my surroundings. My 2003 surroundings with gas guzzlers that resembled big ugly bubbles lining the street and men in suits walking briskly to the corner, where overhead subway tracks carried the obscene trains, their overbearing sound terrifying as they raced along, surely severely damaging to my ears, though I stood a block away. In my world, we had perfected the subway system of New York. Stations were clean and quiet, and the cars had plush seats. However, the drawback was that only the wealthy could afford to take them.

We waited a few moments before anyone came to the door. Desmond rang the bell a second time before a woman stood before us in her nightdress, her straight brown hair wet.

"Desmond," she said. "Enter, enter."

Desmond introduced me and she gave me a seductive smile, as if I came there to date her and not to tie her child up in chains and toss him to the angry waves.

"Knute is in his room, as usual. I think he has invented a new game, something about dragons invading the city."

Unfortunately, he's the invading dragon, I thought.

We walked through three rooms before we came upon Knute's locked door. I hardly knew what to expect as I walked in, but a small, skinny blond kid sat at the desk. His body was shrunken – I think he had a disease of some kind – his torso tiny, his head enlarged, and his back rolled over. I doubted he could stand up straight.

He didn't turn but when he finally rose to his feet to greet me, I was speaking with a man with a boy's features, or vice versa, I honestly couldn't tell which. His eyes didn't focus on me and he had a mouthful of teeth that were too big for him, and his mouth remained perpetually open. A pensive, lost look of desperation was on his face, rather than a smile.

"Hello, Knute," I said and held out my hand.

The boy ignored my hand and went back to his desk where he had a large desktop computer and several sketch pads.

"Shelby loves your new superheroes," Desmond said.

He sniggered. "What's not to love."

I asked him if he'd ever seen those superheroes before and how he came to name them Dark and Blood.

"From the mind of a genius," he said as he glared at me.

I was perplexed. This odd little being was surely The Brain. How did he set it all up? How was he ever created, I wondered.

"Do you want to see my new game, *Dragon Feast*?" he asked me.

I nodded my head and looked at Desmond, looking upon Knute as if he were Jesus.

We spent about an hour listening to Knute explain his new game and watching some rather colorful frightening dragons fly across the screen to gobble up children in the way seagulls' rape scraps of food.

I was taking a chance but if my future and my past were all intertwined, perhaps Knute was a vision of some kind, a misplaced soul.

"What do you think the future will look like?" I asked him.

He turned to me, his small eyes staring into me and chilling my flesh. "It will be mine," he said.

"What do you mean by that?"

"This world is naïve."

"Oh," I said. "In what way?"

He laughed almost hysterically. He came close to my face, so close I smelled his foul breath. "You don't know anything," he whispered. "You are a fool."

His computer remained idle while we talked, and he told me how to outwit the dragons. "Outwit the dragons and you just may outwit me."

After about ten minutes, a screen saver appeared. I stared in horror as I focused on my wife, sitting in this little bastard's computer, reading a newspaper in a big stuffed orange chair with a playful puppy at her feet.

Unable to speak for several seconds, Desmond and Knute looked at me in an odd way. Desmond was puzzled but Knute seemed amused. I turned my attention to him.

"How did you do that?" I asked, quietly at first and when he didn't answer. I bellowed, "How did you do that?"

The little bastard hunched up his oddly shaped shoulders and said, "Do what?"

"That's my wife in your computer. She's your screen saver, you little bastard."

"Hey, Shelby," I heard Desmond say, "take it easy."

"Should have taken better care of her then." The little bastard turned off the computer, and in seconds, my wife was gone.

I grabbed Knute by the neck and shook him. "You better

tell me how to get to her," I hollered.

He laughed. "Get to her? You can't get to her. She doesn't really exist, like a holograph doesn't really exist. She's a screensaver, asshole."

I squeezed my hands around his neck tighter. I pulled him out of his seat until he was dangling in midair. I shook him violently and kept squeezing his neck until his face turned blue. Desmond grabbed me at one point and shoved me off Knute. He punched me repeatedly. "He's just a kid, you son of a bitch, you son of a bitch."

Despite the pain of his punches, my eyes locked on Knute jumping up and down and clapping his hands as if watching a fucking clown make faces at him.

"You little bastard," I kept repeating as Desmond dragged me out the door.

CHAPTER THIRTY-FOUR

I had two black eyes and a bloody nose, and my shoulder was killing me where Desmond had gripped it the whole ride back to Manhattan. He yelled and screamed and called me a crazy man and shoved me out of his car when we got to Shelby's building. "Fucking asshole," he said as I tripped out and made my way to the lobby.

I limped past the doorman's appalled stare and collapsed into bed. I think I slept for two days. When I awoke to sun streaming in the bedroom, I shuffled into the bathroom and stared at Shelby's pathetic reflection. His eyes looked like sad little wounded slits in his face and his bloody nose resembled a mushroom omelet with ketchup.

I showered and dressed and just as I was tying the shoelace on one of Shelby's designer Nikes, the phone rang. It was the demolition guys calling to tell me they had found the concrete unit, and did I want it torn down. "No," I screamed and ran for my car keys.

I got up to Pindar Corners in under two hours and went straight to Nobody's Road. It was beautiful when I got up there, well, all except for the concrete unit. The views were miraculous. The crew had left for the day, but I saw a lone figure sitting on the ground looking around as if he'd found heaven.

I stared at him for a while, wondering what he was doing there, when he jumped to his feet and lifted out his hands. "Wow, Shelby, this is beautiful. My mother told me you bought the land."

I almost fell over; I was staring at Steven Cordova as a young man. He walked to me and gave me a hug. "How are you doing, Shelby?"

"You don't know me?" I said despondently.

"Of course, I do. Shelby Morton."

"I knew your father."

"Oh, I didn't know that."

Shit, shit, shit, I thought, he doesn't know who the hell I am. "Ever hear him talk about Harry Cooper?"

"I didn't know my father."

"Right, right. You didn't." I paced as he watched me. He probably thought I was losing my mind.

"Listen, Steven," I began. "Did your father leave you a key?"

"To what?"

I sank to my knees. It was over. There must be another way inside that unit. I stared at it. "I have to get in there," I said and pointed to the storage unit.

"Okay."

"No, no, I really have to get in there. Adina needs me to get in there."

"Who's Adina?"

I sighed deeply. I couldn't answer that question without being hauled off to the loony bin.

"Someone close to me," I said.

"Oh. Well, congratulations on buying the land. Good move, I'd say. You can build up here. You'd have to get rid of that piece of crap first, but you could build something spectacular."

I nodded my head and shook the hand he held out to me.

"My mother said you should come for dinner."

"Yes, of course," I said as I watched him walk down the road. He turned. "Hey, you don't need a key for that storage unit, someone broke one of the windows."

Scared to believe my good fortune, I could have jumped up and down on the ground. I ran to the unit. The broken window was high, and I'd need a ladder to reach it.

"I need a ladder," I said.

"I've got one in my garage. Come on, we'll go to my place."

I drove to Steven's house and we shoved a ladder in the back. I put a flashlight through my belt loops. When we got back to the unit, I was smiling: I'd be able to save Adina from dying too soon, then maybe I'd rip the whole place up.

But I was too late. I jumped through the window and shone my flashlight around the empty space. Everything was gone, the server, the wires, the computers and the fucking holographs, all of it, gone.

I climbed out of that fucking dungeon and I threw myself on the ground and wept. Steven sat by my side. "Why don't you tell me what's going on, Shel?"

I told him. I told him all of it, every bit of it, starting with my pursuit of his daughter and my re-emergence as Shelby Morton. I told him about The Brain, about the Computer Project and about the horrible boy who made a screensaver out of my wife.

After the two hours it took for me to get all of it out, he put his hand on my shoulder. "We're doomed, Harry," he said. "I believe you. Sadly, I believe you. I do suspect we're doomed."

"You're a big part of my life, Steven," I said.

"I need to think about all this. Do you mind if I just take a walk?"

"Sure," I said.

He was only gone a moment. When he returned, we sat for about twenty minutes, his arm around my shoulder. It was so still, so beautiful. I never expected the silence to be broken, to be shattered.

"I'm sorry," Steven said.

The ambulance came rushing up the hill. Instead of wanting to kill Steven for not believing me, for calling the crazy posse on me, I simply felt defeated. I let them pick me up and place me on a stretcher and carry me into that fucking white screaming van.

I cried out for Adina, over and over I cried out her name as the van rushed over those country roads with the speed of a jet plane, as if they couldn't get me locked up in the looney bin fast enough. I cried out for Adina and I continued to cry out for her, until she finally answered me.

"Harry," she said.

CHAPTER THIRTY-FIVE

"Who are you?" I looked around the barren room. I was in a bed and there was a television across from me. An old woman gazed at me with a soft smile.

"Harry," she said. "Welcome back."

"From where?"

"I'm not sure. I prayed for you to speak to me, but you remained silent for so long, and then I suddenly dropped my purse on the floor. It made a noise, and you opened your eyes and tried to sit up, as if the noise had startled you. Oh, Harry. I have prayed for this."

"You can't be my Adina. She doesn't pray. Nor is she old."

A puzzled look crossed her face, tinged with sadness.

"I have to get up to Pindar Corners, I said."

"Where's that?"

I looked at her in horror. Yes, she was familiar. But it couldn't be, I thought. But the more I stared at her, the more I realized the terrible truth. "Give me a mirror," I said.

"Oh, you are still as handsome as ever, Harry."

"Give me a mirror," I repeated.

I stared at my face, my old haggard face, my wispy grey

228

hair. I looked at my hands, veined and thin, my fingers gnarled. The brown spots on my face and hands looked as though they had been stained with drops of coffee. I put the mirror down and wept. Adina held me in her arms.

"When did I get old?" I asked.

She laughed softly. "We got old together. I stopped looking and when I looked again, we had lost ourselves to time."

"I must get up to Pindar Corners," I said and tried to rise. "Could be the fountain of youth."

"I don't think you are in any condition to go anywhere."

"I am getting up now. Do we have a car?" I tried to rise from the bed. "Shit," I screamed.

"How can you go anywhere … you can barely walk."

"Shit," I screamed again.

"Aging is not for sissies, Harry. Get hold of yourself."

"Wait a minute, wait a minute. What year is it?" I asked. "3006."

I fell back. "He changed the date, he must have."

"What date?"

"The year of your death, it had been earlier, but I spoke to your father. He must have somehow changed the date. Maybe it was your grandfather who did it."

"I don't want to know when I am going to die, Harry."

"Yes, of course," I said and took her hand. "Please, let's go to Pindar Corners. The answers are there."

"What answers, Harry? I don't think there are any."

I looked across the room at the orange chair. The dog at my feet awoke and lifted his head. He was old now too. I stared in horror at the fishbowl across the room and the little lone fish that swam around and around its tiny universe.

Oh, my God. I was a screen saver too. I must be. "How long have we been here?" I asked.

"We've been here forever, Harry, but at least we have television."

"We're screen savers."

"Yes, I know. He added me first. Then he added you, but you were not awake. He made you sleep so we couldn't speak. Now perhaps he's in the mood for chatter."

I looked at her despondently and she returned my devastation with her own.

01.001.1.1.001.1.01.1.1.01.1.0001.001.1.01.1.1.1.01.1.001.0001.1.1.1.001.001.001.1.1.01.1.1.001.1.001.00000001.01.001.001.1.01.1.1.1.01.1.00001.01.1.001.00

We spent days, weeks, years in that tiny universe. We got even older, but we didn't die. Not even the fish or the dog died. I knew we had to escape. I lay in that bed until I figured out how to do it. How to shatter that little bastard's prison. We had a bathroom. At least he gave us that, a bathroom and a tray of food each day. He probably heard every word we said, but the bathroom was private.

I didn't think he'd want to hear our bodily functions, so I took to writing on the wall, to communicate with Adina. I asked her if she knew where the screen was, and she wrote back that she thought it was to our left. She said she saw a sliver of light, every now and then, light possibly coming from the screen when the computer was turned on. I waited until I saw it for myself. I told her we would wait until the computer was dark and then I would pick up her chair and smash it toward the screen with the intention of breaking it. We would then escape.

Adina wrote on the bathroom wall that I was a genius.

We waited patiently for the little bastard to turn off his computer. With difficulty, for Knute was on his computer constantly, but then one night, Adina roused me from sleep.

"It's time," she said.

I picked up the chair, which was not very substantial, swung it behind me and slammed it forward with as much strength as I could muster. We heard the glass break and saw sparks flare, but we leapt through it.

We leapt into darkness, but we raced forward. We ran and we ran. I held Adina's hand and I heard her breath, felt her legs beside me. At last, we were there, at Pindar Corners. I was young and she was young, but we were not flesh and blood. We were holographs in a theater, actors on a stage and all around us were men and women, smiling from their chairs.

"Bravo," they screamed. I looked at Adina and she looked back at me. I reached out to touch her and nothing met my hand. "Bravo," they screamed again. "Bravo."

PART IV:

THE LAND
OF DARK
AND LIGHT

CHAPTER THIRTY-SIX

We were holographs, created solely for the pleasure of The Brain. We had little control over our movements, for we were now part of a chess game controlled by computer. We moved across the chessboard by command of signals from beyond, controlled by minds we would never know.

There were others in this strange universe. Adina and I were Bishops but there were also Rooks, Knights and Pawns. A board filled with chess pieces controlled by the passionate concentration of madmen. It felt like five years, but it might have only been one. We were moved sometimes slowly and sometimes quickly. We had no will to move ourselves. We didn't eat or sleep; we moved toward the finish until were tossed in the air. But then, out of nowhere, something happened, and the world went topsy-turvy and we were freed from our confinement to a watery grave, plunged out of nowhere into the dark abyss of an ocean.

Somewhere in the far distant stasis of our air, I heard my father's voice. "Hang on, Harry," it seemed to say, a misty far away drone. "Hang on, Harry." And so, I did.

We came to the surface in what was once New York City. Adina and I climbed up on a lone block of wood and looked out across the Atlantic Ocean.

"But the oceans all dried," I said.

"No, they returned, giant swells, a giant volcano, geat tsunamies."

The ocean had swallowed everything. We swam down to the bottom and found the city among its watery grave. The chess pieces we had known floated past us. Computers were everywhere, waterlogged and silent they swirled. Our bodies slowly formed, and we were again on the surface, sitting back on the block of wood.

"Are we dead?" she asked me.

I didn't know the answer.

"I have to get to Queens," I said.

She looked at me in astonishment. "Why?"

"I have to break his neck," I said softly.

The Skycars flew above us, proof that the world had gone on, that New York City had perished but the Skycars still flew. Not all was lost.

He's still breathing," I said. "And as long as he is, the world will suffocate."

I heard her sigh. I didn't know if she were human. I'm sure she wondered what bile I was made of. I stood to my feet and pulled her up. "Which way is Queens do you think?" I asked.

I watched as she searched the world around her. She looked like a ghost trapped in a vision. She took my hand. "This way, Harry," she said.

CHAPTER THIRTY-SEVEN

But there was no Queens, no Queens, no Brooklyn, no Bronx, only the Atlantic Ocean and the little block of wood we'd found to sit on. So, the little drone I had known as Knute was dead. Or he wasn't yet born. Who knew?

"Pindar Corners?" I turned to my wife. "Do you think it still exists?"

"Nobody's Road," she whispered. "It began there, and it will end there. Somewhere there's a car to steal and a road that isn't underwater. And when we get to Nobody's Road, we choke the life out of it. The indifference, the technology, The Fucking Brain. We choke the life out of it, Harry."

"Progress?" I whispered.

"Fuck it," she said.

We made it back to Pindar Corners by the grace of the soul file's God. We had come upon cars that weren't locked, people who weren't speaking, a world of unbearable silence. All the while my mind was churning. I thought of old Mr. Wilkens and his hobby, fish bombing. He had loads of dynamite. I thought of blowing that concrete eyesore off the face of the earth. He would help me, I was sure. Either that or I would steal the dynamite.

Mr. Wilkins was not there to offer me dynamite but we would not be defeated. His garage was filled with it.

I took the right-hand turn on to Nobody's Road. I had stolen the dynamite from Mr. Wilkens' garage. I was sure he wouldn't mind. He was nowhere to be found and this was an emergency. We would destroy every computer, every wire and every piece of communication in that goddamn piece of shit. I had Adina wait outside.

"But Harry, I want to be a hero, too."

"My darling," I said. "In my eyes, you are and always will be my hero."

She pouted in that silly way of hers. "Leave Mr. Wilkins a hundred dollars," I said. "I have nothing on me but a few twenty-dollar bills printed in 1980."

"Is that his old, rusted truck?"

I looked over and saw the old orange and brown antique vehicle driving right at me. He brought it to a stop a nanosecond before making a pancake out of my body. Mr. Wilkins got out of the car, his face beet red.

"You stole my dynamite," he shouted. "I saw you leaving my garage, I saw you from the cow field."

"Mr. Wilkins, I did steal your dynamite, but it is for a good cause. You must help me. You have an opportunity to save the world."

"Are you out of your mind? Hand it over," he said.

I shook my head. "I can't. I have to do this."

"What are you trying to do?"

"Blow up that unit behind me."

"You can get licensed blasters for that. You don't need my dynamite."

"I do, I do need it." From over Mr. Wilkins' shoulder, I saw my Adina creep up behind him with a shovel raised high above his head.

"Run, Harry," she screamed as she brought the shovel down on his back. Poor Mr. Wilkins stumbled to the ground.

I ran to the unit and climbed inside. I set the dynamite in the center of the unit and in the back of the unit as well as the front. My hands were shaking as I set up the explosion. I set the timer. I did not have much time, so I leapt from that concrete slab of hell just before the explosion ripped through the sky. I threw myself on the ground as large chunks of concrete fell around me.

When I opened my eyes, the explosion had left nothing behind. There was nothing left. It was as if it had never existed. Had it taken me with it, I wondered. Is that why I can't see it?

Adina took my hand to her mouth and kissed it.

01,001,11,001,1,01,1,11,01,1,0001,001,001,1,01,1,11,01,1,001,1,0001,11,1,001,001,001,11,01,1,1001,1,001,0000001,01,001,001,1,01,1,11,01,1,00001,01,1,001,00

My father stood before our house at Pindar Corners. I saw him for just a moment. He gave me a thumbs up. He smiled at me before he vanished.

I was lying on a road, my chest covered in blood. My wife's tears fell on me.

"Don't die, Harry," she wept. "Please don't die."

I smiled at her. "Are they all dead?" I asked.

"No, my darling. It was an accident, a hunter. No one else has been shot but you."

"Where am I?"

"Hawthorne Road. You've been wounded." She began to cry again.

"The Brain?" I asked. "Did we kill it?"

Her eyebrows knotted, and she looked confused.

"Did we kill it?" I repeated.

"Don't speak, Harry. The ambulance will be here soon."

"I have to know. Did we kill The Brain?"

She bent to kiss my cheek but didn't answer me. But above me, I saw birds and around me were children, their laughter carried in the breeze like music. The air I took in was so sweet and clear. It was my last breath. But I understood that whatever The Brain had been, he'd been defeated.

I was dying under the bluest sky I had ever seen and the last face I saw was hers. I was a hero. The world was restored for better or worse and I had seen to it. God gave the world its soul. I thanked him for that.

Adina tried to hear what I was saying. How she would tease me if I told her I was thanking God. She cradled my head in her arms and rocked me. I smiled just one more time for Adina before I left.

THE END

www.ingramcontent.com/pod-product-compliance
Lightning Source LLC
Chambersburg PA
CBHW020134120726
47903CB00007B/2256

* 9 7 8 1 6 4 4 5 6 5 7 7 3 *